D0458970

steer

toward

rock

ALSO BY FAE MYENNE NG

Bone: A Novel

steer
toward
rock

瑨

FAE

MYENNE

NG

HYPERION

New York

Illustrations/calligraphy by Linette Lee Atar
Designed by Cassandra J. Pappas

Library of Congress Cataloging-in-Publication Data is
available upon request.

Steer Toward Rock is a work of fiction. Names, characters,
places, and incidents either are the products of the author's
imagination or are used fictitiously. Any resemblance to events
or persons, living or dead, is entirely coincidental.

ISBN 978-0-7868-6097-5

Hyperion books are available for special promotions, premiums,
or corporate training. For details contact Michael Rentas, Propri-
etary Markets, Hyperion, 77 West 66th Street, 12th floor, New
York, New York 10023, or call 212-456-0133.

FIRST EDITION

10   9   8   7   6   5   4   3   2   1

致父親

伍錦炎親

蔡有信

尊敬

紀念母親

張杏芳

In honor of my Father
In memory of my Mother

I

report

報
告

昭

THE WOMAN I LOVED wasn't in love with me; the woman I married wasn't a wife to me. Ilin Cheung was my wife on paper. In deed, she belonged to Yi-Tung Szeto. In debt, I also belonged to him. He was my father, paper, too.

The Father bought the Szeto name and entered California as the legal son of a gold miner. After he made his fortune with a run of gambling houses on El Camino Real, he was called Gold Szeto. Who can say if he intended to send for his barren first wife, but with the money he sent home I was bought into the family.

As a child, I was taught to pay respects to the Father's passport photograph, which was set on the Ancestral Altar. When I asked why the Father's image was placed next to the dead, the Mother told me it was a plea for his return.

I was nineteen when he wrote for me to join him in San Francisco. Even now, more than half a century later, when I light a match to my cigarette, that slight singe reminds me of that day I walked out of my home village as the first Japanese bombs fell. And with every woman I have loved, I have also feared her eventual sadness as I recall my last image of the Mother, her face aslant and her shoulders trembling in unrequited love. Finally, I can understand that her placement of the Father's image next to the dead was for hope. Her weeping was her knowing surrender, her husband would never return.

When I sailed, I knew that I too would not return. When the S.S. *President Coolidge* landed, I stood on the dock and watched my fellow passengers step into boats headed for the Wooden House on Angel Island. When my name was called, a man stepped forward and drove me to the Department of Justice where the Father and his lawyer waited and I was admitted into the country as the blood son of Yi-Tung Szeto.

The Father's greeting was to inform me: I listed you as a married man. One day, that immigration slot will be used to bring in my Replacement Wife.

Gold Szeto was the only Father I had, so the law of family was my rule of blood. Obligation and Obedience, this was my Confucian curse. I weighed the consequences of disobedience and I accepted the two-year term. He said in that time, my fake marriage would dissolve and I would have bought my life back. I believed it. Time was my trusted currency.

They say a child of seven plays with abandon, that a boy at fourteen enters a realm of wonder and a man of twenty-one explores through the erotic his possible immortality. By twenty-eight, every man should have standing in the community: a wife, a family and a good name. I was a year away from the height of manhood and I had little hope for these three joys.

Joice Qwan was the woman I loved, the one I wanted

to call my intimate one, the one I wanted to protect. But she was a Bamboo Woman, born in San Francisco and bred with western wind. She didn't understand what I wanted to give her.

For her, I entered the Chinese Confession Program. I wanted to be my own man. For love, I confessed that the Szeto name was false and I lost my citizenship. I gambled that Joice would interpret this act of independence as my declaration of loyalty. But she wasn't interested in my gift and in the end, heartache shadowed me and I would learn the reach of passion, the grip of rancor and the profundity of regret.

I cut meat then and what butchery taught me was that the body was the only truth. As blood flowed, it tracked heat till the veins cooled, till the beat broke. In death, no man is common. In death, every man becomes a god. A simple man claims his boldness by blood but the superior man expresses his humanity with tears.

Would I cry?

Yes.

Would my tears stain bamboo?

Yes.

Would my heart be cut?

Yes.

I never wanted to be the hero but I would pay its price and never enjoy its victory.

Yes. I was almost loved. Love almost came true for me.

曙

I WAS a butcher. What a man did with his hands spoke
his worth, so I tell my livelihood before I tell my name.
Jack Moon Szeto is the name I bought. This is the name I
made my life by. San Francisco was my port of entry. Sail-
ing in, the Golden Gate Bridge looked so wide, but when
the ship was directly underneath, its narrow shadow surprised me. As I listened to the cars roaring in both direc-
tions and felt the pull of the ocean as we neared shore, I
hoped for new roads.

I read meat. I moved my fingers through marbled flesh
like a vulture's beak, I fanned muscle from tendon and
found by feel the soft flank that was gold. I angled my
knife tip under the head of a vein and yanked it out like
coarse thread. I glided blade along bone so that flesh
peeled away like petals of magnolia.

I was a Master. Between palm and thumb, my grip was
firm. My aim could sever a whistle. I knew the flat metal
smell of decay. I ran with the dead-cold on my shoulders,
I heaved while bearing dead weight. I knew that surrender

was a color, a sudden odor, a certain give. All day the band saw whirred in my joints and all night I felt its humming along my forearms. As a butcher, I wanted to harness the stroke that cut through bone; and as a man, I wanted to speak to the mark. If there was a promise I could not fulfill, I did not inconvenience others by talk. No man wanted to taste another man's swallowed desire.

Yi-Tung Szeto was the man I called Father but that was only my mouth in obedience. I was registered as his son in the American courts and blessed As His Blood Born before the Ancestral Gods. For my papers and passage, I was four thousand dollars in his debt.

Every man needed an ancestor and every ancestor needed a descendant. Paper or blood, I paid my respects. Every New Year's, I visited the Father with sweets and good wishes. Every Harvest Moon Festival, I delivered a box of double yolk moon cakes and on the solstice, I brought the Father a sack of winter oranges. This was the proper ceremony and I performed it.

Gold Szeto gave me my livelihood and I am grateful. He started me out as Bird Boy at his Universal Market. Selling live birds was allowed then. Fresh-killed was preferred because it insured the potent transference of healthy properties. The Universal carried the best selection: hens and roosters, capons and pullets, squabs and quails. Ducks, all kinds of mountain birds, sometimes even the rare ring-necked Manchurian pheasant. I worked in the garbage alley, a tight square space where I could only turn one revolution. The bird crates were tucked behind the door, a gas burner over a small table leaned against one wall, a large garbage can against another. When a customer ordered a bird, I reached into the crate, grabbed one, ripped off a patch of feathers and slit its throat with one pass of the blade. After I drained the blood into a bowl, I threw the limp bird into the garbage can where it thrashed. I turned the water to high and had a cigarette. When the bird was still, I pulled it out and held it in the boiling water just long enough to loosen the skin. Then I plucked. The work was all stink, blood and feathers and feces, the stench scraping like a blade up my nostrils. I started plucking at the head and yanked all along the tight wing feathers around to the downy underside till the bird was clean and smooth and bald.

My lot was as bald. Yet I wanted to be like the rooster, common as salt, but glorious with his five virtues. The rooster wears a crown, he has dignity. His spurs are sharp; he is a hero. He is brave; he faces his foe. He is generous and communicates when he finds food. A rooster is trustworthy; he tells perfect time.

I was a man who sold my sweat. I relied on my own abilities and I did what I could with my own hands. I never made trouble for anyone and I did not believe in wastefulness. A working man should not aspire to drive a Benz. A common man should not expect favor from a great beauty. What I could not have, I did not crave.

I lived as if in a chicken cage. From the Universal, my world extended only a few blocks in each direction. I worked on Washington, had a room at the Waverly Arms on Waverly Place, ate breakfast across the street at Uncle's, dinners at Great Eastern and, when I fancied, a midnight bowl of noodles at Sam Wo's.

Every Friday, we were prepared for the City's health inspection, but one Thursday an inspector walked in without notice and measured the distance from the bird alley to the butchery and declared the Universal in violation of the Hand Washing Ordinance. Then we were all required to wash our hands whenever we crossed that imaginary line separating beef from bird. When Gold Szeto finally calculated how much time each butcher spent at hand washing, he ripped down the ordinance and cursed their fake law. But soon enough, the inspectors returned and this time they shut down the Universal.

Gold Szeto sent me around town to work off his debts. I spent two winter months shining shoes in the Square and discovered that whores approached men in daylight as boldly as in the night. In the dungeon of Chong's Hand Laundry, I scrubbed away stains and spit-starched enough shirts to outfit an army for Mao's Hundred Flowers Campaign. My perspiration became so salty it stung, and the intensity of colors made my eyes ache.

The basement galleys of Chinatown's tourist restaurants were the worst. Every kitchen was white and hot and fist-tight. Men who worked with fire had no patience and were more territorial than the Japanese Imperial Army. For the seven months I worked the fry station at Ocean Palace, not one night passed without the Master Cook drumming his cleaver and cursing everybody's mother.

Woks ablaze, cleavers athunder, fire made fire.

How many wok-wars started over a mis-peeled garlic clove or a too-thick slice of onion or a chunk of celery? The Master Cook's temper added up as if on an abacus. I learned to count the beads of heat on his forehead, I learned to read the swelling vein at his temple, thick as a forefinger. I became skilled at throwing my shoulder into his bulging chest, punching my elbow into the carotid that surrendered his last exhale.

Then I was sent to Happy Palace where I prepped for the cooks. I tore lettuce as delicate as a woman's earlobes. I wrapped wontons into seashell shapes. I stirred and picked bone silt out of the broth. When I chopped vegetables, I arranged them by size and shape, so that I could parboil the stalks before the leaves. I peeled onions and garlic and cut scallions into slivers. I sliced carrots so thin, the edges curled. My lotus root and turnip slices were so transparent, I could read the farmer's almanac through them. But it was my hearing that became my most refined sense and the sound I dreaded most was the thud of steel sinking into flesh.

The Fairmont was my last assignment and I discovered that I liked being out of the kitchen. I mopped marble stairways, polished brass and waxed parquet floors, and let my mind empty onto the vastness. When I made beds, still moist, still warm with scent, I wondered about my own happiness. I was no longer soothed by the arrival of light or grateful for the cover of night; I felt like the world's unluckiest bat.

Gold Szeto took advantage of the shutdown to rearrange both blood and business matters. The Universal would reopen six months later as Chinatown's first full service market. Cabinets and shelves were built for imported goods and two twin refrigeration cases were ordered for the new vegetable section. Gold Szeto had foreseen the growth of the community and contracted farmers in the Delta to grow specialty vegetables and the first crop of baby bok choy arrived with the sudden burst of newcomers. Opening day, we handed out shopping bags for each lady, tea and sliced fruit for the children, cigars for the men. Customers admired the remodeled butchery, the modern fishery, the roaster, the barbecue hut and the long shiny takeout counter.

But the most significant change was the arrival of two sons, men who not only bought into the Szeto name but also his business. Brother One became the roaster; Brother Two, the fishmonger. I hadn't paid off my debt and could not afford to buy a partnership so I asked permission to learn the blue touch. Gold Szeto hesitated long enough to make me feel that this was a great generosity.

Regardless, I expressed my gratitude. Irregardless, the Father charged another five hundred.

For interest, he said.

As you dictate, I said.

SO I LEFT the Bird Alley and became an apprentice butcher. I worked hard to repay my debt and I also earned a reputation. Next to Fat Gee, Eight Digit Gorman and Master Cleaver, I was the favored. All the ladies fought to be served by my hand. I was the only bachelor butcher.

From eight to eight, I stood under an ashy brightness that cast no shadows. A dampness lined my brow as I looked over the chrome cases into the wanting irises of so many new brides. My heart ached as I watched those hopeful irises fading meal by meal. In the beginning, when the new wives prepared for the monthly visits of husbands who worked the farmlands in the Central Valley or construction in the Southland, they insisted on inspecting the marble of each slab of meat.

But hope was a voracious lover. I witnessed how the empty bed consumed each lonely wife. When those irises flickered at me, when their voices trembled, when they ordered chuck instead of flank, ribs instead of lean pork, pig hoof instead of oxtail, I knew love was lean. And when they stopped ordering their monthly lamb, I knew they were resigned to being *grass widows*, like the forgotten wives left in China who only dreamed of their husbands.

Every first Tuesday of the month, a wife in green came in for a lamb heart. She waved the other ladies ahead so that I could serve her. When she took her package, her hand always lingered to graze mine.

Why lamb? I wanted to know.

Lamb warms the blood, she told me. My husband works in Alaska and when he returns, he needs the heat.

She also told me she worked at Wonder Café and the day I went to see her, she wore a bamboo-patterned dress under her floral apron. When she brought me coffee, I asked why she favored green.

Green is for money, green is for life, she said.

I waited while she closed the café and then carried her groceries back to her apartment on Himmelman Lane. She made me a dinner of several lamb dishes and I stayed the long warm night. After, whenever I saw her walking into the Universal, I would pick out the freshest heart and have it wrapped by the time she was up to my station.

Lily Way from FourFiveSix Noodle House served me extra dumplings and after closing, we went into the storeroom, where the sacks of flour were tall and the smell of yeast was strong. The twin Jue sisters from the soy factory favored me with special tofu desserts. With Lai-kay, the night manager at Chinatown Bazaar, with Landa Gong from the telephone exchange and in the Wells Fargo vault with Meikum Lam, I enjoyed their need and their reprieve.

I was the Lord of the Peach Blossoms, lucky in the garden. Many asked to be my sweetheart, but I swept them away when I met Joice.

畓

I FIRST SAW Joice Qwan at King Duck's Noodle House. Mankok and I were running a hand truck of butchered pigs to the Four Seas and as we passed, there she was, sitting at my favored table. Soup fog misted the big windows, so I couldn't see her face well. I was drawn to the way she held her bowl, a thumb on the top rim and four fingers beneath, so that the heavy restaurant bowl seemed cradled in her palm. There was a luxuriousness about her every move; when she swallowed it was as if she was consuming a precious tonic, not just a common chicken stock.

Let's go! Mankok shoved me. Don't dream about her, she hands out towels at the Underground Bathhouse, sells tickets at the Great Star Theatre. Don't lust after her, she's dirty. Day and night, old men throw wolf-eyes at her. And worse than dirt, her mother cleans corpses!

What's to be afraid of? I asked.

You want to be the brave hero? Go and drink her tea, eat her dumplings that her mother kneaded after washing corpses. Remember! This loyal brother gave you warning: Her mother touches the dead.

Don't we all? I asked.

AFTER DINNER, I went to the Great Star. There was a line of movie-goers so I waited under the marquee. In the ticket cage, behind a window of wooden slates, Joice looked like a captured bird. She sat under a bare bulb and her hair fell like a loose sleeve across her cheeks. Every few minutes the small oscillating fan blew her hair back and exposed her wide forehead. I thought she could have played the tragic heroine instead of selling tickets to *The Dream of the Red Chamber*. Her face had Lin Dai-Yu's triangular beauty: her chin a soft point, her forehead as smooth as a newborn's and her eyes had a quiet that I wanted to trust. When I walked up to the ticket cage, her eyes snapped onto mine like magnets. Then she looked away and cranked the fan so that the air blew straight into her face. Relief softened her bold features and I wanted to reach through the cage and cup her diamond face in my hands.

I slipped my bill under the slot. She looked up and smiled, Don't you cut meat at the Universal?

I do, I said.

Then she pushed my bill back through the slot and said, I'm treating. You're the only butcher who will serve my mother, the only one not afraid to touch her hand.

Her eyes were still as an oath I could not decipher.

Go in, she said.

After I told her that I hoped to return the favor one day, I walked across the red lobby, pushed through the double doors and entered the darkness to watch the last half of *The Dream*.

*   *   *

A FEW NIGHTS later, going home after a late game at Edso's, I saw her on Powell, walking along the top of the cable car tracks. I watched as she kicked one foot in front of the other, her wide coat sleeves cupping in the wind. She stopped at the exchange plates where the two tracks converged and bent over and pulled up a metal bar.

When I walked up and asked if she wanted to make real trouble, her eyes lit up like festival lanterns. If she was surprised to see me, she didn't show it; if she was alarmed that a man approached her in the night, she didn't seem unaccustomed to it.

She handed me the bar like a sword. Show me, she said.

I yanked till it snapped, then threw it over onto the other track. Wait and watch, I said.

We walked around the corner and slipped in the foyer of Cumberland Presbyterian Church. The night air was still. She stood so close, I felt her liquid warmth.

I listened to the gears scraping and then the brass bells ringing and the wheels rolling, and then came the sound of singing.

It's the new motorman, she whispered.

Suddenly there was a huge boom like an ocean liner crashing and the singing became cursing. She took my hand and we ran down the hill, laughing like schoolchildren. Like a refugee, I glanced back once and remembered how destination had to be more important than any desolation escaped.

As we passed Four Seas, the Pacific Telephone Exchange and the Three Gold Emporium, my footsteps matched my heartbeat and I felt like a ghost in her trust. I followed her up Washington and onto winding Old Spanish Alley till she stopped in front of a makeshift door, two crimson-painted planks, entry and exit nailed together. She had trouble working the padlock so I stepped up.

Let me, I said. When the door gave, she took my hand and pulled me into the dark. In the corridor, I saw the faint glow of cement and almost made out the courtyard beyond. She turned to me with her liquid eyes. Behind her, the gas meters glowed like foreign clocks. A strand of hair fell across her face and when I tucked it behind her ear, I felt her softness and my heart ached. Then she leaned her cheek into my palm and I cradled her head as she sank into my grasp, her weight and warmth soothing me.

Her coat fell open. Come, she said.

Yes. I pulled her in.

She moaned, the tips of her lashes a brushstroke against her pale skin. I touched her lobe, pinching the porcelain flesh. She offered her neck and I ran my tongue along the tight tendon that throbbed. Her eyes poured into mine and I felt myself dissolving.

The fog had thickened. Every surface pulsed with wetness. Her cheeks, her lobes, even her lips were cool.

This? I slipped my hands inside her warmth.

Her eyes glowed like fired stones.

I pulled and skimmed against her heat.

More? I asked.

Yes, she moaned.

Yes.

I followed her rising breath. I held mine.

Then all of a sudden she turned and threw herself at me. I fell against the can, she kicked it away and I was against the brick wall. She yelled out something and I yelled out something else. I pushed back. She pushed harder. Then we were rolling along the alleyway pushing everything, making a rolling racket. She kept yelling.

I heard a window pop open, a voice call out.

More! Joice yelled again. Then she pulled away, running into the courtyard, into a stream of moonlight. Like a flame extinguishing from a match, she was gone. I saw a flip of skirt, a twist of ankle. I lit a cigarette and thought, Joice was my ghost of love, better chased than caught. Then I listened to the flat clack of her heels on the cobblestone, the sureness of her footsteps up the wooden staircase, and I knew, this was a woman who was not afraid. Joice Qwan would make her own road.

Her scent lingered in that wet dark and I took it in. I waited till I heard that hollow click, that distant turn of lock, a sound made more intimate because I knew she would not come out again, and then I walked out of the dark corridor and let two shut doors divide us.

坥

THE NEXT MORNING, I went to the Underground
to find Joice. It was hailing so I lifted one side of the
metal trap door and stepped down into the dungeon. She
was alone, reading at the counter. When the wind rushed
through and rustled her paper, she looked up.

You didn't tell me your name last night, I said.

Joice.

Joice? Like the alley? I asked.

She nodded.

You don't have a Chinese name? I asked.

Ling.

Ling? I wrote the character on my palm. With the jade
radical and command character on the right? I asked.

She touched her jaw and told me Ling was the sound of
two pieces of jade touching. Her father had named her and
she had liked how he said it. Then she started school and
was teased, so she'd changed it, taking Joice from the alley
where she was born.

She looked so uncomfortable, I changed the subject

and asked her how many jobs she had. When she put up two fingers, I counted the two things I liked about her, how she bit her lower lip as she read, how her lashes fell straight down like a tiny wing.

She opened her palm and said, Fifty cents.

I'm not here to bathe.

She took the towel back. Then what?

I want you to have dinner with me tonight.

She smiled.

Yes, I said.

Then she reached over and tugged at my earlobe. As quick, I caught her wrist. She twisted but I kept a firm grip and felt her blood rushing through that narrow gorge of bones. I pulled her close enough to feel her hot breath on my face.

I let go and said, That's a yes?

Tell me first if your ear was pierced with a hole puncher, she said.

Come with me and maybe I'll tell you.

Smiling, she went back to folding towels. Then she shook her head. I can't.

I stood there looking at her a while. No problem, I said. I'll ask you again.

I WOULD KEEP visiting her at the Underground. Strangely enough, unlike my first visit, we were never alone again. There was always a steady stream of old men and they all brought some kind of treat: black coffee, black bean cake, pork bun or a taro dumpling.

Most days after work, I helped Joice close the Bathhouse. Usually when I arrived, the fans were already turned to high and the faucets were all tabbed to hot. The Underground roared like a slice of ocean. Joice would be sweeping out the rooms. I flushed the toilets and scrubbed them. She poured bleach into the tubs. I scrubbed those too. She hosed down the showers and I mopped the cement floor. The fumes were astringent. The steam was a cloud of pain. But when our eyes met in the foggy mirror, I had hope.

While I dropped off the dirty towels at Sun Laundry, she tallied and recorded the day's earnings. I brought back the clean laundry and stacked the towels, she switched off the hot water and the fans, locked the cash and ledger into the drawer and then we climbed the stairs up into the last of twilight. Above ground, she slipped the padlock on and snapped it shut and said, The Underground is closed, my day is done.

One day, I heard the fishmonger telling her about the first delivery of Dungeness crab and saw how her eyes lit up. After closing, I suggested we go to Four Seas.

She talked more than she ate. The first thing she told me was that since her father died of a heart attack six months ago, every old man who came to bathe wore her father's face.

You're the youngest to walk down into the Underground, she said.

The young don't soil easily, I joked.

She looked around the restaurant and said, They hold a lot of wedding parties here.

It's best for seafood, I said. Chef Hoy is a master with crabs.

My mother is home tonight, otherwise, I would have to cook for my brothers, she said.

Day off? I asked.

No funeral scheduled, she said. Tonight, no family weeps.

Why don't you work at the bathhouse in the South Ping Projects where the women and families go? I asked.

Stupid family stuff, she said.

Then she shrugged like it was more than simple pain so I didn't pursue it.

The Underground is my Uncle's place and I'm working there to repay him for my father's cremation costs, she said.

So the dutiful daughter was conscripted?

Her slow laugh hid something, but I didn't know what. Cremation is unusual for Chinese of his generation, I said.

She shook her head. I can't remember the fight, but cremation was his concession to my mother. They both came to me with the decision as if telling me notarized their anger.

Angry about what? I asked.

She shrugged, What weren't they angry about?

Chef Hoy's crabs arrived with an egg sauce that slipped like gold into the crevices of the cracked claws. I placed one on her plate but she just looked down at it. So I cracked it and pulled out the pink flesh for her.

She put the fleshy limb into her mouth and sucked the sauce. This is so good! She smacked her lips. If I were home, my mother would be listing the price of each dish like a recipe: five cents of pork, thirty of beef, a nickel bag of soy beans, each morsel flavored with copper and nickel. And she would be talking about the last wake, every night, the new dead was a guest at our table.

And your father?

He worked as a cook at the Starlight Diner in Gilroy and only came home every six weeks or so, she said. Every summer, he picked me to spend the summer with him. I waitressed and kept all my tips. He slept on a cot in the kitchen so that for three dusty months, I got away from the noise and the trouble of home.

The vegetables came and she helped herself to it heartily. I love hollow spinach, she said.

What did I think? I thought her anger at her parents was odd, that her personal grievance was not useful. I liked that she had a good appetite, was not shy about enjoying her food and then I thought about our differences, that she liked her rice sticky and I preferred each grain separate.

After dinner, we walked up to the little park at Pagoda Place. The fog hadn't come in yet and the air was windless, dry, no bite, no chill. I saw an old man cast a fish eye on Joice as she walked ahead of me.

Goodnight, Old Uncle, I said to him.

Long night, he replied.

Joice and I sat on a bench watching two brothers playing handball. A few gas lamps flickered above the empty volleyball court. The shadows of the buildings fell, wide as huts over the parked cars on Sacramento. We sat, listening to the slow bouncing ball, to the boys' voices. We watched a bum enter the park. His arms were wrapped in newspaper and his legs were tied with sheets of cardboard; he shuffled one revolution around the court, checking the garbage cans before leaving. A young mother hurried by, a sack of groceries in one hand, a child in another and on her back an infant in a cloth-cradle.

That was my mother, Joice said. But it won't be me.

A window creaked open, a voice called out to the boys.

Joice took my hand and held it up to her cheek.

I asked, Are you always this familiar with men?

Her voice changed. I was with someone and my parents made a lot of trouble about it.

When she started telling me about her affair with a cable car brake man, I was uncomfortable.

He was black and married and had three daughters,

the youngest my age, she said. He was good to me, he believed in me. He listened to me. He took me seriously.

The four mandates of friendship, I said. But I didn't tell her what I really thought. It was an old story. I surmised that he was the first to tease her away from the family fold. I agreed that her parents' opposition to his being black was unfair and I suggested that because they were not educated, the coarseness of their disfavor was understandable.

But not forgivable, she insisted, and she wasn't ready to stop.

While she talked, I listened to the thumping ball. I understood she was thrilled to discover the power of her body and that she had never imagined the physical could possess such pleasure, having only witnessed her parents' physicality as laborers. I agreed, It's good not to be afraid.

Never, she said.

Another shout, this time a man's firm voice came from above and the young brothers ran off.

We were alone now. I thought about how to get away from hearing her story.

She continued talking as if to herself. When Willie worked graveyard, I'd sneak up to Taylor to be with him. We did it on the trolley, the wooden benches were like ice sheets. We sneaked into the cable car barn and did it next to the giant cables whipping and snapping, with the odor of burnt oil, the spark of scraping metal.

Weren't you afraid, wasn't it dangerous? I asked.

She only smiled.

I wondered if being so close to all that high voltage had harmed her.

She continued, On that stone bench by Taylor, in that garden above Vallejo and then behind the Condor on the lower Broadway steps, that was the last time, that was when my father saw us.

She stopped talking. I tried to find words to comfort her but I couldn't think of any so I took her into my arms. Don't do this to yourself, I said. Don't make yourself so sad.

囍

JOICE AND I BECAME friends by the clock. At seven, we met for breakfast at Uncle's Café, and again at seven we met for dinner at the Great Eastern before she started her shift at the theater. Near midnight, I picked her up and we stopped for congee or midnight noodles at Sam Wo. After, we'd come back to my room. The heat and charge of our sex gave me a peace. The first night I walked her home, Old Lady Qwan was at the door, ready with a pelting of harsh words.

The old woman wagged her finger and yelled at me in her professional wailer voice. Your mother feared that son-snatching ghosts would steal you! She fired the silver cap of a chopstick and stamped it through your lobe and pierced you like livestock to anchor you to the living! But you are doomed, you're bad luck!

Then she turned and yelled at Joice. The son who is pierced has misfortune to deflect! A boy raised by a mother in fear is not the man for you. Do not be seduced by his sad story. Do not believe touching the boy will make the man bloom. That is only for a mother to do! She slammed the door.

We stood there for a long while and then walked till we ended up at the cable car barn where the loud banging of metal and rubber covered over the harshness of her mother's words.

What story? Joice asked.

Your mother believes my background is unlucky, I said.

Why?

Gold Szeto is not my real father so there is no security if you go with me.

Then, who is your real father?

I shrugged. He's the one I call Father; he's the one I owe.

And I thought I had it bad, she said, shaking her head.

Her pity didn't surprise me. It's hard to explain, I said.

I THOUGHT about it after I walked her home. Joice was seven years younger, which I felt was a good distance in time and experience. My hope was that she could see me as a protector and I could nourish her as a treasure. A few nights later, she came looking for me at the Buddha Bar, clearly upset so we went outside and started walking. I smelled the moisture from the trees and said, It's going to rain.

I like rain, she said.

Water released something in her. Let's go to Coit Tower, she said. Then she started telling me about why she had to get out of the house.

I was helping with dinner, making the meat patty, chopping the water chestnuts, mushrooms, sausage and salted turnip. My mother kept saying superstitious garbage about you and then she brought up Willie. I drummed my cleaver just to drown out her voice. Then I slapped the meat patty onto a plate, that onto a steaming pan. I turned the gas onto high till the steam started escaping and I thought of all my mother's words evaporating. Then I left.

Joice's voice turned pensive. She doesn't even remember that you were the only butcher who was kind to her.

Kindness does not ask for payback, I said.

On the top of Telegraph Hill, we entered Coit Tower's stone lobby. Joice walked straight up to the mural of an old couple holding hands, walking down a garden path. She said, That could never be my parents, not with their arranged marriage.

Don't you have any friends you can talk to? I asked.

We're friends, she said. We're just talking.

We circled the lobby once more and went outside. The rain had stopped and the air had a crisp edge. I heard crickets.

My father and I had a bad goodbye, she said.

I lit a cigarette and said, It wasn't your fault. Your father was a man of his time, he spoke the worst in order to invite the best.

You don't know, she said. The last time I saw my father, I was with Willie. We had been dancing at the Condor and came outside for air. It was a warm night. I sat down on the lower Broadway steps. Willie was all angles, a triangle from cheek to chin, clavicle to belly. I pulled him down to me and we started doing it. Then I heard something that was like keys. A *tink tink* floated my way; I felt I could almost see the sound. In my mind, I saw the jade pendants that hung from my father's belt. Then I remembered it was his weekend home, and this late he must have parked on Broadway. In shock, I looked down and my hands had a bluish tinge from the fluorescent lights and I saw them on the darkness of Willie's chest. I pushed him off. That's when I caught my father's eye and I felt the full force of his disappointment. Then he looked away and I was alone in my disgrace. The doors to the Condor opened and loud music filled the street but all I heard was my father's metallic taps clicking away. He went back to Gilroy and less than a month later, had a heart attack and that was it.

We started walking. Down Telegraph, I smelled night-blooming jasmine. We passed a loquat tree and I plucked a pale pear-shaped globe and handed it to her. I wondered if her father had not looked away, might she be able to forgive herself? But the old-world father, either in his pride or to spare her shame, had looked past her in hopes of saving her. To her western eye, she felt driven away.

What I recognized was a person in grief—loss or gain—all was the same color. If her father had lived, would he have taught her that desire was not a road to knowledge, that love was never ideal, that yearning was not hope?

As we turned onto upper Grant, I heard a swing of sound, a tangle of keys. I finally understood. When she had been reluctant to tell me her Chinese name, I had assumed she was ashamed. But it was because she hadn't trusted me. In the family fold, the name felt intimate. As jade must be worn close to the skin for its protective heat, she'd tucked her name away to keep it safe.

We passed the white church and crossed Vallejo. She led me into a café and we sat down at a long table with many other people. By the entrance was a phone in a tall wooden box, the door was shut but I heard a woman crying. Joice ordered raspberries and then talked about her summers in the central coast when she first tasted the tart and sweet fruit. She smiled as she remembered how her father had described the tiny plump berries. They pop in your mouth like a scoop of fish eggs.

I found her sincerity touching. I tasted sweet followed by a quick unusual sourness and that's when I felt the first ache of losing her.

畓

OUR CLOCK TICKED forward and I believed we were walking one road. At Sam Wo's one night, the stools were stacked on top of the marble tables and the smell of chlorine was coming up from the lower floors being mopped, Joice asked who my real father was. I told her I didn't know and that it didn't matter.

What about your mother?

I had three brothers, I said.

You were the youngest?

I nodded. They taught me to swim, I remember that.

Ocean? she asked.

River.

That's not so hard, she said. So what's your real name?

This one, I suppose. The one I use.

Is it your favorite?

Favorite? I don't think like that, I said. Then I told her about my contract with Gold Szeto.

What are you talking about? A man can't have two wives! she said.

He can, I said. He does.

That's breaking the law, she said.

Family law, I said. He wants a son.

That's sick, she said.

I'm going to ask him to release me from the contract.

She looked away. Do whatever you want, she said.

Right then, I felt our roads dividing.

眢

WHAT WAS IT I felt the night I found Joice waiting for me in front of the Waverly Arms, what was it I wanted when she gave me this news without salutation or any sense of elation?

I have, she said.

To have happiness was to speak about new life. But she left out the word *happy* and I felt empty.

The light was muted but still strong enough to cast car shadows onto the sidewalk. As we walked into Pagoda Park, young boys slipped ahead. We watched them set up the volleyball net, their voices like the hard teeth of a comb pulling through hair, their hands firm as the knots they tied onto the poles. They yelped as the white ball flew straight up into the air.

We have happiness, I said in confirmation. I'll talk to Gold Szeto.

She looked at me with eyes as defiant as I'd ever seen.

So we can marry, so we can be a family, I answered.

What for? Her voice was as hollow as the white ball

that bounced toward her. She got up and kicked it. I never said I wanted that, she said.

As the boys dived under the ball, I counted how many hits kept it afloat. I listened to the ball bouncing back and forth and felt my own fading heartbeat. Then what were we doing? I asked.

I'm not in love, she said.

What did she mean? I had no idea. I understood love to be a shared fate, a feeling grown from seed, a flower eternally beautiful. I had no idea what she meant. When she talked about being surrendered in feeling, it sounded as unpleasant as being in a wind canyon. So I got up and walked to the last bench and I kicked at it till it knocked over. Then I just stood there, eating wind, upset at her, upset at myself, lost in a storm of impossibilities.

I heard her call my name but I didn't turn because I was afraid to show my eyes, I was sure they would be misunderstood. I knew this moment would complete her: the girl was gone and the woman had decided, what to suffer and what to sacrifice. This moment would define me too, I knew what I said or didn't say would proclaim me the lost man. So I left her there in the park and walked down to the Avenue. At the row of noodle houses, Lily Yick at FourFiveSix was counting bills over the open register. Next door, King Duck's was shut down. The soup caldrons sat on the counter like oversized helmets, the dark woks hung above the stove like ancient tortoise shells. At Happy Palace, workers squatted on their chairs, knees clasped to their chests like a school of vultures waiting for Big Wong's hands to deal out cards. The men waved, their raised palms flat as if still balancing plates, their banner smiles broadcasting their hopes. I waved back, my hand turning yellow and green as it slipped through the neon ribbons from the restaurant sign. I envied how these men could throw hope out like dice. Gambling unified them, gave them the strength to forget their fatigue and boredom. After a day of labor, the common man used money to chase off the next day's hunger. A game of pigeon cards could hold his focus, numbers could fold him into a sanctuary, a home where he could forget. If only I could lose myself in that sort of dream.

As I passed Shanghai Rose, a Lincoln pulled up and the concierge held the tall doors open and piano music drifted out like a bunch-up of bamboo chimes which somehow softened my anxiety. How to make Joice see my hope?

A motorcycle roared past and I was transfixed with the way the girl pressed her cheek into her boyfriend's back, how her arms wrapped around him as if in deep sleep. I watched her hair fly by like a page of night and I longed to be held in the kind of trust.

But when I turned the corner onto Waverly, the wind slapped like Joice's last bitter words. *I'm not in love with you.*

眢

THAT DELIVERY THURSDAY, we were one butcher short. It was already after six when the Fanelli Brothers pulled up to the Universal so I knew it would be a long night. Franco made no confession of the refrigeration trouble when he swung open the doors and I held my comment about the faint whiskey edge of rot; it was the third day of an October heat wave and we had to get the meat into storage. The brothers quickly set up the rails, hooked the collars of beef and began shoving them off the truck. Mankok and I grabbed the flanks, ran the carcasses back to the big freezers. As we dragged the empty hooks back, they jangled on the wires like warning bells and that's when I noticed a man watching me from across the street.

Mankok whispered, Gold Szeto's new messenger, a Hakka, you don't want trouble with him.

I walked across Waverly to greet the Messenger but he wouldn't shake my hand. He only delivered his message: Gold Szeto wants you at 850 Jackson.

I studied his face. It was meaty and square and when

he spoke, a long scar pulled at the corner of his lip so that it looked as if he was swallowing his own words. From his long O's and his clipped V's, I heard that he wasn't a native son of the Four Districts. Looking into his eyes was like looking into a cloudy mirror, my own worry reflected back to me twofold. I didn't know what Gold Szeto wanted and I was trying to figure out what I wanted. I wanted Joice but she didn't want me. I was willing to risk whatever I needed to get free so I could have a chance to be a family with Joice. Though she said she didn't want me, I believed that if I could do something to show her my sincerity and intent, she would change her mind. I trusted she would see the sense and logic and return my love, I wanted her love in the family way.

Gold Szeto is waiting, the Messenger repeated.

I pointed at the truck and said, Delivery was late.

Suit yourself, he said and turned to leave. I studied how the Messenger's shadow absorbed into the ground, impressed with how nothing broke his pace. I vowed to be as determined with Gold Szeto. As I unloaded the lamb and pork, carried in boxes of hooves, bones and cold meats, I resolved not to let fear derail me, and by the time Franco and I were dismantling the rails, I decided that regardless of what Joice said, I would steer straight toward my goal and I would ask Gold Szeto to release me from my marriage contract.

Saturday? Franco handed me the invoice.

I reminded him about the refrigeration problem.

No delivery charge? He smiled.

We shook. As I guided his truck out onto congested Stockton Street, the dry heat pressed down on my head, heavy as a flatiron. Back inside, Mankok prepped for the restaurant deliveries and I cleaned the butchery. I scrubbed the chopping boards, removed the blades from the grinder, cleaned and then reassembled them. I sharpened all the knives, rinsed them under a jet of water, oiled and slipped them back into their wooden slots. Then I went out on the selling floor, wiped down the glass display cases and polished all the chrome counters. After sweeping up the clumpy sawdust, I opened a fresh sack and scattered it over the ground like seeds. Then I untied my bloody apron, called out a good night and left the Universal.

Washington was shut up tight as a tank. The sidewalk in front of the fishery was hosed clean, the window shades of Ho Wan Pastries were drawn and Moy's Sweets was padlocked. The sky wore a dark sleeve of river and the stars were blinking through, slow as carp. Down on the Avenue, only the Buddha Bar was lit and the jukebox music spilled out like thrown dice.

The closer I got to 850 Jackson, the more the building looked fake. The roof tiles were too orange, the four corners lifted up like exaggerated smiles and the dragons crawling up the pillars looked sinister instead of benevolent. But this was an assessment of my own predicament. I wanted to approach Gold Szeto as a new world man, but I felt powerless against his old country hold. In China, Gold Szeto would only be a common crook, but here in the Flowery Kingdom, there was not even a name for his brand of thievery.

A man called out my name. Not once, but twice. I turned to see Fourth Fong from Fong-Fong Brothers Ice Creamery waving furiously.

I have news for your Old Man, he said.

What's so urgent? I asked.

Tell Gold Szeto that the INS came and asked about him.

Asking what? I kept my voice flat so as not to excite him.

The usual. Is Szeto his real name? Does he own the Universal? What's his relationship with Jim Mulligan?

You tell him, Fourth was loyal, Fourth looked out for him. Then he pushed out his chest, and declared, I told them nothing.

Heard you, I said and walked on. The vermilion doors at 850 were locked so I went around to Jasper Alley.

Brother, I greeted the Messenger.

He was friendlier in his own territory and said, Gold Szeto's been waiting.

When he took my extended hand, I recalled the saying, Today adversary, tomorrow kin. I thanked him and headed up the staircase but when I heard the lock bolt behind me I realized I had no back-up plan.

On the mezzanine, I looked down into the dry goods emporium. In the center was an island of wooden barrels, the largest ones filled with rice and millet, the smaller band of barrels containing the red and green mung beans, ginkgo nuts, almonds and lily bulbs. As I stood over a hundred thousand seeds, I bemoaned the fact that I did not have one grain of choice in my life. A dim bulb flickered in the corner, its dull light as cautious as a rat's pupil and I asked myself, What would I sacrifice? I looked into the center island at the feast of shapes: there were disks of dried scallops and medallions of oily oysters. There were sugarcane stalks, anise stars and cinnamon twigs, flattened squid, seaweed sheets, and tangles of black moss. From this bouquet of brine and bark, from these peppery extracts and pressed blossoms, I cultivated my resolve to be fearless. I wanted to make my own family. That was my truth.

As I stood at the base of the steps, I thought about the secret half-floor Gold Szeto had built between the mezzanine and office, and I smiled at his cunning. When it was illegal for Chinese to own property, he had Jim Mulligan purchase the Universal and 850 Jackson as well as four rental properties in the Western Addition. In exchange, the Irishman was as shrewd, insisting that a secret floor be built for his stock of scotch. So this had to be the root of my inspiration. If Gold Szeto could break the law and still protect his holdings, I could be man enough to break family-rule. If Jim Mulligan could be shrewd enough to lend out his name in order to protect his assets, I would follow suit and protect myself.

When Gold Szeto remodeled the storage attic into an office, he had the door cut short and narrow to accommodate his slight stature. To enter, I had to duck and turn sideways as if slipping into a cage. Two steps in and a long desk made from a single length of yellow camphor blocked me. Its surface shone like water and its circumference could not have been wider than a girl's waist. Gold Szeto sat, still as a tombstone dog.

Your Fake Wife arrives in two months, he said in greeting.

In welcome, I said, Joice is pregnant.

His eyes were as hard as the dirt that packed salted eggs. You're already married, if that's what you're asking, he said. And I already told you, after two years, I'll pay for your divorce and you can marry Joice then.

What I want is to take care of Joice and the baby. I want a chance for my family, I told him.

Silence filled the room like a sour tonic. Gold Szeto wouldn't look at me, he looked out the dark pane of windows. I watched his hawkish profile and waited.

If it's a boy, I will raise it. As my son, he will not lack, he said.

I asked, What if a daughter? Our night-eyes met on the black glass.

If that's the case, you could give as much as I, he said.

There's nothing more to say then, I said, and started to go.

Come back! he demanded.

We met at the door and I said, What is it?

If Immigration Officers come into the Universal or stop you on the Avenue, tell them we are Szeto. We are true father and son, you are my blood born.

I looked at his high forehead, I saw his thin brow twitch. Is that all? I asked.

Don't mention that I send money home to the True Wife.

Are you afraid they will brand you a communist for sending money home?

He continued, If the INS comes around asking about our family's loyalty, your answer should be that we stand behind the Generalissimo.

I smiled and said, I will tell them I am only loyal to my rice bowl. He clenched his teeth. I waited but he said nothing more.

What I say or don't say won't be of any consequence. No doubt the Americans already have a case on you, I said. Then I passed on Fourth Fong's message.

Heed, he said again.

That's when I knew I had a small victory. Repetition was his mistake. Repetition highlighted his true fear. I left without a farewell, having faced my own fear. Outside, I also knew I had just made my own trouble and there would be no victors. On the dark cold avenue, I felt like a cut man, hoodwinked by my own fear. The metal taps of my shoes echoed on the empty avenue, one click hopeful, the next click hollow. A strong wind rattled a broken plaque above the Buddha Bar. I looked up and saw a bed sheet blowing like an abandoned flag. On the lamppost, I noticed a new bulletin. The characters *hon pak* were on the left corner and the golden seal of the eagle on the right. I ripped it off and put it in my pocket.

A sharp wind blew and I walked against it all the way to the Great Eastern Café. Four foreigners burst out just as I reached for the red doors, they called out hellohello! like a song. Inside, I passed a few old men at the counter reading the paper. Booths lined the wall like a dining car of the Southern Pacific. I saw Louie Yue and slid in.

Why are you sitting with your back to the door? I asked.

He shrugged. I'm not afraid. Why so late tonight?

Gold Szeto called me to 850, I said.

He offered me a Chesterfield and then said, From your expression, I say it wasn't too good a meeting.

Never is, is it? I lit up.

Edso brought me a glass of tea and said, No fish delivery today.

Beef and soft tofu, I said. Those foreigners tip?

Tip my head! Europeans don't give dog shit, said Edso.

Not their custom, I said.

They should respect the customs of the countries they are in! Edso said.

Do you? Louie asked.

Then they should eat at Shanghai Rose, Edso said.

Louie scoffed, Chef Tang's dishes taste like dog vomit.

Tell Sifu Hom not to use so much oil, not too much salt too.

No oil, no salt, no flavor and you no complain! Edso shuffled off like a cloth-slippered house girl.

Bad mood, Louie winked. His wife ran off to Texas.

By herself?

Who eats such luck all alone? With that waiter Liu Bei, from Ocean Palace.

The one with the drippy nose? I asked. We worked

together, he got fired the first night because he mopped himself into a dry corner. Bad enough he didn't know better but then he had to go and cry.

He's smart now, Louie smiled. He's eating happy now.

How much did Edso lose? I asked.

Nine big lumps. No-brain hid the cash in his mattress, Louie said.

Edso set down a bowl of house soup and then rocked back on his heels. There's a game at Gene Gee's tonight, he said.

No money. I drank my soup in one swallow.

Edso threw his chin at Louie. You! You're smart at poker. How about I give you one bit and you play, win or lose, four parts is your share.

Louie rapped twice on the table. Your butt! I play one bit for nine back.

Edso threw up his arms and walked off.

Louie said, There goes the Grand Master of the Boiling Water Sect.

What kind of master? I asked.

The Master of Coolies, Louie said. Look at him, rushing right, rushing left and bumping into everybody. No one wants to work with him. If I gave him a hundred thousand, he would still be waiting tables. That's why his wife left, his sort doesn't know how to eat the good life.

As I listened to the thumping of the old fans and the rocking of the woks in the kitchen, I thought about my friendship with Louie Yue. Ours was a history of days off, days of fun, days of being free. We met when we had adjacent rooms at the Waverly Arms. Evenings, he bartended at the Buddha and his days were for pure enjoyment. He laughed at those that rushed between jobs, drinking lukewarm tea in between. On days off, we caught crabs off Aquatic Park and had them the raw drunken style. Many

nights, we left the Forbidden City near dawn. Other evenings were spent at the Rickshaw Club or playing pool at
Lambert's Hall. Louie was good at pool but better on the
two-stringed violin. At the music clubs on Wentworth Alley,
even old men got teary-eyed listening to Louie playing
"Twin Moons Reflecting on the Lake."

Louie was called the Orchid King. He had fierce eyes,
a warlock hairline and a jaw like a long knife. Women
said his smile was intoxicating and they couldn't take
their eyes off him, those that never drank came to the
Buddha Bar every night just to take in his heroic splendor,
first sipping red wine and eventually finding solace in
brandy. Though Louie would enjoy his garden of wil-
lowy women, tradition released no man and one day an
aerogramme from his Old Mother arrived to announce
that she'd had him married in a ceremony using a rooster
as proxy.

I was about to ask about that when the bells jingled
and the front door opened and a well-dressed black couple
entered the café. From their dress and elegance in manner,
I knew they had been dancing at the music clubs along
Kearney. They waited by the door and Edso moved toward them, the dark sheen of his uniform shifting slow as
mud. He led them to a booth directly across from ours and
handed them menus. The woman held hers upside down,
so I caught her eye, made a flipping gesture and she turned
her menu right side up.

Why such a long face, Louie wanted to know.

I'm in a bind. Before I could make my request, Gold
Szeto made his.

That's how it always is, Louie said. You pull out your
gun only to find a bigger one pointed at your nose. What
do you want?

I don't want to play out the fake marriage.

Louie laughed. How many more wives before he believes his jade stem doesn't work?

Two years. That's the term, then we divorce.

Two years is a pot of tea. Is she yours in this time? Louie asked.

That's not my dream.

I'd take a taste, he smiled.

I bet you would.

Is she pretty?

I saw her photo, she looks like a city girl.

Hong Kong girls are trouble but our local Bamboo girls are worst, Louie said.

The bells jingled again and a parade of boys marched in. They were dressed in black jeans, white T-shirts, tan suede tie-up boots, front-zippered jackets with sharp collars and sleeves cut off just past the elbow. They wore their belt buckles to the far right, closest to the favored hand. The last one to enter seemed to be the leader. He was the tallest and had the longest hair and because he held his head at a tilt, he appeared shy. Then he started down the long aisle, moving slow as a bride, glancing left and right, his hip popping slightly, his gait rolling, the ball and heel of his feet in a consorting dance.

Hoodlums, Louie said. That one in black is the Big Cake.

What about those in brown following him? I asked.

His Crumbs, Louie said.

Big Cake muttered something and all the Crumbs broke out in laughter as they passed the black couple. I thought it was rude and felt embarrassment for everyone involved.

Louis sighed, Like you, my good life is ending. My Old Mother and the country wife will be emigrating.

What will you do?

I'll enjoy myself now, Louie smiled. You should too.

Joice is pregnant, I said.

Louie looked at me and said, Normally news like that calls for congratulations but I don't see much happiness in your face.

Joice doesn't want it.

Louie smiled. The baby or you?

I paused. Both, I suppose.

You have a problem then, he said.

Her thinking makes no sense.

It's easier to get rich than to understand how women think, Louie said.

Edso set my plate down. The beef had an incandescent sheen, the tofu was seared but still soft, the chives were bright, the garlic roasted and the ginger had a tang but I had no appetite. What can I say to make her understand? I asked.

Maybe she'll say yes if you are a true American, Louie said.

I showed him the flyer I yanked off the lamppost. You mean this?

You could, he said. If you enter the Confession Program, you confess you're not his real son and then Gold Szeto has no power. No fake name, no fake wife, no problem! Joice will see you as a hero and might even marry you!

What about the money I paid to buy my papers? I asked.

How much?

Four big lumps, seven percent interest.

He shrugged. Not a small bit, but that's all gone.

That's it? Gone?

Brother! You broke the law.

That law was not fair, I countered.

Fair is no one's duty to you, Louie said. I wouldn't complain; someone might let it slip that you have a fake name and the government will come and pressure you! If you confess, they have the right to deport you, but if they don't deport you, you can get naturalized.

Why naturalize? I asked.

To be a citizen, Louie answered.

What for?

To vote. Vote and change the law if you feel so righteous.

How can I do that? Gold Szeto brought me over, he gave me a livelihood. Gold Szeto will never agree to it, I said.

You paid him back already, Louie said.

Labor and interest, I nodded. He promised me a partnership, but when the time came, it had a price.

Then there was a commotion and I looked over and saw the black man throw down some bills. He stood up, took his woman's hand and they walked out, as elegant in exit as they had been in entrance.

Edso brought out the platters of food and started cursing the empty table. The hoodlums demanded to be served their food and as I listened to Edso naming and presenting each dish as a gift, I wanted to follow the black man out into the street and apologize for the hoodlums but I didn't. I failed to respect a fellow man and I would have to live with my regret, I was my own brand of hoodlum. I felt for the black man, a stranger in this Chinatown eatery, with no friend to explain the rules or blood kin to protect him. It was the same for me. I thought about what I owed Gold Szeto and wondered, How much repayment was enough?

It wasn't over. The Crumbs were emptying the condiments onto the table and making a paste with tea. Louie told them to stop, but they only laughed. When they got up to leave, Louie blocked Big Cake and said, Your first point of rudeness, I let go without comment. Now you are disrespectful to your own and I cannot ignore that.

Big Cake threw out his lip. What was the first point?

You were rude to the outsiders, Louie said.

They're black! Big Cake countered.

Do you like being disrespected on the outside? Louie demanded.

Big Cake glowered.

I would expect that the son of Ray Ginn should have better manners, Louie admonished.

Big Cake's jaw set. Then he threw his arm up and a Crumb-boy left some money and they all flew past like horseflies, the door clanging after them like a dropped bell.

As the boys walked by, I noticed the gorilla stitched on their right seat pocket. I also saw that only the Big Cake had a perfectly hemmed sleeve. The others' sleeves were raw, frayed, threads hanging down like spider legs. How tough was the Big Cake if his were the only sleeves to be stitched neatly? I asked.

Louie laughed. He's probably got a mother who works in the sweatshops. How would it look if she let him leave the house with a raw seam? Cut sleeve, frayed sleeve, it's all the same. Every hoodlum has a mother to fear as every hero has one to revere.

I have nothing to fear, I said. Joice already said No.

You're right. You're already cut, Louie said.

So I'll enter the Confession Program and then offer myself as a true American and then Joice will want me.

How romantic, Louie smiled. Confession as proof of love and loyalty.

I got up to pay my bill. Who knows, she might accept it.

There's no telling, Louie agreed.

At least I will have tried my best, I sighed.

We stopped at Beckett Alley and Louie pointed at the view of the full moon sandwiched in between the tall buildings and said, Only a few more hours till sunrise, let's not sleep it away, let's drink it away!

A barmaid stepped out of Red's Place and beckoned to him.

Louie kissed her and waved for me to follow them. The moon toad is out, so the dawn will be tremendous! he shouted.

Another time, I said. I have too much on my mind.

Don't think too much, Louie said. Life should be fun! A muddled heart never leads the hero to a new dawn.

True, I said, shaking his hand. Good night, good brother.

智

EVER THE GOOD FRIEND, Louie didn't make me feel hope where hope was not available; he let me grieve so that hope might be renewed. He took one look at me when he came into Uncle's and said, Time for squirrel wine!

I told him, Joice said the sun was round and I heard the sun was square so it was impossible to fit ourselves into one sentence.

Louie laughed, Didn't I warn you that too much worry led to talk and too much talk led a man to his last dead end? Talking won't do it, women can talk the sun into setting. Nothing changes, we men are still sitting in darkness.

Who doesn't want a family? I asked

She doesn't, she told you that twice, Louie said.

She knows I care about her, that I want to take care of her.

Are you deaf? Now I'm telling you, she doesn't want you. Bamboo Women love to drink wine, they have a hollow inner stem that makes them blow this way and that.

She says No now, but tomorrow, she might scream Yes! Bamboo Women love to sway between the extremes.

I can't sleep in a storm, I said.

We China Boys have to root or we rot, he agreed.

Only a Fool needs to hear that twice, I said. How many times should a man repeat himself before he is the beggar tapping his own empty bowl?

Louie got up and paid. Time for squirrel wine! he repeated. Brother, you have a love malady! But Louie's Chevy wouldn't start, so we took the cable car downtown and caught the Number 21 Hayes. At Golden Gate Park, we walked through the long meadow, past the buffalo pasture and eucalyptus grove onto the lawn near the Arboretum. We used peanuts to lure squirrels down from the trees. When one got close, I trapped it with a pine branch and Louie knocked it out with a large flat rock. I put it into a brown bag to carry it out of the park and we got back onto the bus. But the squirrel was only stunned, it soon woke and struggled to get out.

A white haired lady scowled at us and we moved to the back of the bus but she reported us to the driver who threw us off on Polk, so we walked the last mile back to Chinatown. We slaughtered and gutted the squirrel in the alleyway and then took it upstairs to the communal kitchen and skinned it. Louie went to his room and came back with a gallon jug and packets of herbs. After he slid the pink carcass inside the jar, he threw in a fistful of red dates, a palm full of knobby roots, slices of dark bark, chalky slabs and pinches of dried bulbs and nuts till the squirrel carcass was buried under bark and blossoms like a forest after a heavy rainfall. He counted out the slices of ginseng, precious pits and wai-shan, which he noted was for the extra enhancement of squirrel powers. Last, he emptied a whole jug of the wine into the bouquet, shook the jar to coat everything and then screwed on the lid.

Who taught you to make this? I asked.

My old man.

What kind of sickness did he have?

Broken heart, Louie said.

When I told him again that Joice didn't want the baby, he lit me a cigarette and said, Don't start building the great false wall of hope! Don't be a coolie of love!

She didn't like Gold Szeto's proposition, I said.

I wouldn't either, he said.

But I want my child.

That's not up to you, Louie said.

I watched him write the date on a square of red paper and tape it onto the jar. I was eager to consume the squirrel properties of speed and ingenuity. How long? I asked.

Nine months at least, twelve would be better.

I counted up till the winter solstice, when Joice would give birth. Maybe Joice will be finished with her anger by then, I said.

One hopes, Louie said.

I did hope.

畓

I DIDN'T ACT. I hoped so hard that the day Gold Szeto came and told me to supervise the delivery of the marriage chamber, I heard one gate shutting with such a clang that I knew it would never open again. I lost my freedom.

Wayne Alley was so short it wasn't even listed on public maps so that when the city replaced the old gas lamps with electric lampposts, it wasn't listed on the work orders. It was also one of the only alleys that didn't burn down in the fires after the Big Quake. The new street sign read Wayne for the tourists, but we called it Kerosene Alley for when oil shops lined the cobblestone lane. An old store sign still hung in the bend: One can, one dollar, one week of light.

Wayne was also the only alley that dead-ended twice. The first was fake, a wall of cinder blocks to stop cars from using it as a shortcut through to California Street. Then the road curved and turned to cobblestone and ended at the real dead end, my white clapboard building. I climbed up to the top floor and opened the door and found myself in the kitchen, in the sum of white. Stove, refrigerator and table, each appliance was a cube, every corner rounded, every surface polished. Beyond the kitchen was a large square room with a couch, two soft chairs and a lamp on a low table. The bedroom had one small window and the paint fumes were so strong, I opened the window and then went out to the landing to wait. When Chun Lung arrived, I helped unload and carry the frame and posts upstairs and we assembled it. After we brought up the box spring and mattress, we threw on the crimson bedding and then stepped back and surveyed the marriage chamber, the carved bedposts were like handmaidens and the brocade cushions were as shiny as the irises of the blind.

There it is, your throne of joy. Chun Lung smiled.

Or my prison, I thought. I asked what he thought about confessing.

Hon pak? He shook his head. Never! I'm not crazy! They've been sending someone around, bothering my father at his laundry, my wife at the noodle factory, even my distant uncle; some government worker acting like a Jesus missionary trying to trick us into believing the others in the family had already confessed but the family had a meeting and we all swore not to confess.

THAT NIGHT, I went back to the apartment. The full moon followed me into the alley like a toy lantern. The headlights of abandoned cars in the empty lot glowed and my shadow loomed ahead, leading like a large friend, or a larger foe. From across the way, I could hear the gliding sounds of ivory tiles and the click of the abacus and then the heavy pause before a rip of cautious laughter. This was the business-breath, this was a game between masters and the wager was in gold. I had my own wager; I was gambling my heart and liver.

A strong wind blew and a woodsy perfume announced her. Joice was sitting on the bottom step, still as a seal on a rock, her hands clasped over her knees and her hair poured over her shoulders. I cupped my palm over her crown but she jerked back so quick, my hand glanced off like a spill of water. She narrowed her eyes, sharpening her gaze as if to thread herself through me.

You came, I said and immediately regretted my tone. I had meant it as a pleased surprise, but tucked into the darkness, seclusion gave my tone a severity I had not intended, so I stepped back and lit a cigarette. The flame hissed like a curse and when I leaned into its temple the heat housed my fear, and then inhaling, the heat anchored it.

The foghorns blew a long note. In the shadows, her complexion had a gunmetal cast.

Come upstairs, I said. I want to tell you, I found a way. I can confess . . .

No, she shook her head so hard it was as if she was trying to dislodge something. I only came to tell you, boy or girl, I'm keeping it, she said.

You don't even understand, I said. The Confession Program will give us a new beginning. We can be a family. If I can confess, I'm not bound to Gold Szeto, we can have a new start.

Are you crazy? You confess and they have the right to deport you, but if you don't confess and you get stopped or picked up for any reason, they have the same right; either way, you won't win.

I'm doing this for us, I said. After a long quiet, she spoke and her voice was calm. Do it for yourself, she said. Her eyes were hard on me and I forced my eyes to stay kind.

One glance, one word and we were on another road. For me, there was no repeating my loyalty; repetition would only conquer instinct, destroy true feeling. I had to act. I said, Are you sure?

Yes.

I watched the dark road consume her, my fist clenching and unclenching like my heart beating, like my heart aching. At the end of the alley, she glanced upward and then down. For a moment, I had hope, she was undecided. Return or retreat? But then a siren broke through, a fire truck's crimson light poured into the alley and as quick, hope faded. The alley darkened and Joice was gone.

Upstairs, the electricity hadn't been turned on so I followed a stream of moonlight to the marital bed. That's when I saw why she really came. Joice had carved my name onto the headboard. I traced the rough grooves and realized she'd used a screwdriver. And she carved my blood name. *To Have Trust.*

Joice was the only person I told my true name to. Though her calligraphic hand was as unbalanced as a child's, the intimacy of what she wrote was mature. She was telling me that my name, maybe my life, was a lie. I felt a heat expanding in my chest. I only remember the red covers on the bed, the shine of the cushions and that I couldn't stop until I destroyed it all.

Then I was in the middle of a ruin, breathing like a thug. The red and gold sheets were like coiled intestines and the strewn feathers reminded me of the bird alley. The gauze curtains were slashed. The eye of the phoenix, split. The plume of the phoenix, ripped. The dragon's immortal pearl, cracked. The seascape, rent. This was not a bed of happiness.

Joice's coat was on the floor, the body, shoulder and collar collapsed into itself like a sitting Buddha. I picked

that up, along with the shredded bedding and torn cushions and threw everything behind the headboard.

How much was reversed in one day! I did not want to
comprehend the consequences, so I lay down under Joice's
carved mandate and slept through the night.

When I woke, the morning's harsh light poured in like
paint, the bed was hard as an oyster shell and yet I felt har-
bored in tenderness. I lay in the forbidden bed, in the smell
of paint, among the ruin of my own making, and I knew
there was only one road before me.

CONFESSION

I, Jack Moon Szeto aka Yuo Seen Leung, residing at 19 Waverly Place, San Francisco, California, being duly sworn according to law upon my oath depose and say that I understand I am making this statement to a United States Immigration Officer. I have been informed by him that any statement I make may be used in evidence against me at any time, in any proceeding, civil or criminal, which the Government of the United States may deem necessary to institute, and that I have a right to refuse to say or sign anything. I am willing to make this statement and do so voluntarily, without force, fear, threats or promises of any kind.

I am willing to concede alienage and wish to apply for Suspension of Deportation. I voluntarily surrender Certificate of Identity No. 387046, which shows that I was admitted to the United States as a citizen, and passport No. 362891 issued by the Department of State, Washington, D.C. I have this day voluntarily registered as an alien.

INVESTIGATOR TO RESPONDENT THROUGH INTERPRETER:

I am an officer of the United States Immigration and Naturalization Service authorized by law to administer oaths and take testimony in connection with the enforcement of the Immigration and Nationality laws of the United States. I desire to take your sworn statement regarding your citizenship and your status under the Immigration and Nationality laws of the United States.

Any statement you make must be given freely and voluntarily and may be used against you, or any other person, in Immigration and Naturalization Service proceedings, or criminal proceedings. You have the right to consult a lawyer of your own choice, and the right to refuse to answer any question, if you believe that your answer may incriminate you. Do you understand?

A: Yes I understand.

Q: Are you represented by attorney?

A: No.

Q: Are you willing to answer my questions at this time?

A: Yes.

Q: Will you please stand and be sworn. (Complies.)

Q: Do you swear that all the statements you are about to make will be the truth, the whole truth and nothing but the truth, so help you God?

A: I do.

Q: What is your true and correct name?

A: My true and correct name is Yuo Seen Leung.

Q: What are all the names you have or been known by?

A: My Immigration-name is Jik Moon Szeto. My true name is Yuo Seen Leung.

Q: When and where were you born?

A: I am not sure about the exact date of my birth; to the best of my knowledge, I believe that it is November 18, 1935. I was born at Kam Hing Village, Kam Long Heung, Toishan District, Kwangtung Province, China.

Q: Of what country are you a citizen?

A: I am a citizen of China.

Q: When did you first enter the United States?

A: I do not know the exact date; I believe it was in January 1954. I arrived on the S.S. *President Coolidge*.

Q: What was your port of entry?

A: My port of entry was San Francisco, California.

Q: Your Service File A17 278 129 reflects that you arrived in San Francisco on the *President Coolidge* on January 4,

1954, and were admitted February 6, 1954. Do you believe this to be correct?

A: I believe it is correct.

Q: In what manner were you admitted to the United States at that time?

A: I was admitted as the son of a native.

Q: What is your true father's name?

A: Respondent does not answer.

INVESTIGATOR (FOR THE RECORD): At this point the subject, Jack Muen Szeto AKA Yuo Seen Leung, is admonished and reminded that he is still under oath. A ten-minute break is issued

HEARING RESUMED.

Q: What is your true father's name?

A: My true father's name is Leung, Chung On.

Q: Who made the arrangement for you to come to the United States as the son of Yi-Tung Szeto?

A: He did.

Q: Who did?

A: My Immigration Father.

Q: I need you to state the name.

A: Yi-Tung Szeto arranged my papers.

Q: How many brothers did you claim to have at the time you were admitted to the United States? That is, how many sons and daughters did Yi-Tung Szeto claim to the Immigration Service?

A: I claimed three brothers.

Q: How many of the three claimed brothers were true sons of your Immigration Father?

A: The two blood sons, they were Jik-sun and Jik-dip.

Q: Where is Jik-sun living?

A: He lives at 9 Himmelman Lane.

Q: Where is Jik-dip living?

A: He lives at 916 Pacific Avenue Apt. 9

Q: Where is Jik-yet living?

A: He never came.

Q: Are you certain?

A: Yes.

Q: Are you a member of any organization, clubs, unions, or associations?

A: Yes, I am a member of the National Butchery Association of America, NABI-CIO and also the Butchers Union in San Francisco.

Q: Are you now or have you ever been a member of the Communist Party or any other subversive organization?

A: No.

Q: Are you willing to surrender your United States Passport No. 6334, to be forwarded to the State Department, in view of the fact you make no claim to United States citizenship at this time?

A: Yes, I am willing.

Q: Do you have anything further to state for the record at this time?

A: No.

PERSONAL DESCRIPTION

Height, 5' 10"
Weight, 175
Eyes, brown
Hair, black
Hole in left ear

DETAILS

SUBJECT was born on November 18, 1935, at Kam Hing Village, Kam Long Heung, Toishan District, Kwangtung Province, China. He first arrived in the United States at San Francisco, California, on the S.S. *President Coolidge*. He was admitted on January 4, 1954, as a derivative citizen son of Yi-Tung Szeto, an alleged native-born citizen of the United States under the name Jik Moon Szeto, at which time he was in possession of United States Passport No. 6334. He has made no trips to China since his entry. SUBJECT resides at No. 19 Waverly Lane, San Francisco, California. He is employed as a butcher at the Universal Market, 812 Dupont Avenue. He is not represented by attorney.

In a sworn statement at San Francisco on February 2, 1965, attached as Exhibit A, SUBJECT confessed that his true name is Yuo Seen Leung and made no claim to United States citizenship. His immigration father is not related to him. SUBJECT has no true brothers or sisters.

SUBJECT identified members of his false family.

Immigration-father
Yi Tung Szeto aka Chow, Chun On (file A7 147/198)
An alleged native-born United States citizen, but actually born in Ai Long Village, China, and a citizen of China. His case being investigated by Federal and local authorities.

Immigration-son
Jik-sun Szeto aka Chan, Li Shan, (file A7 149/251)
Lives at 9 Himmelman Lane, San Francisco, California.

Immigration-son
Jik-dip Szeto aka Lowe, Wing-sun (file A7 223/354)
Lives at 916 Pacific Avenue #9, San Francisco, California.

Immigration son
Jik-yet Szeto
Slot created, never used.

SUBJECT stated that he is not now and has never been a member of the Communist party. He disclaims any arrest. Local and national agency checks did not reveal any derogatory information. SUBJECT appears amenable to deportation proceedings and is prima facie eligible for adjustment of status under Section 249 of the Immigration and Nationality Act.

習

ON FEBRUARY 2, 1965, I walked into 100 Sansome Street without representation and confessed my illegal entry into the country. I should have left Sansome Street feeling victorious, but I was only more uncertain of my future. I did not know what consequences would arise if Gold Szeto discovered my actions and I felt more lost than ever, in the back country with no compass on law or love.

As for Joice, distance became an easier measure of patience. I stayed away from the Underground even when I heard she had quit. I did not go to the movies at the Great Star and I avoided Pagoda Place. When Old Lady Qwan came in for her soup bones, I treated her as I always did and if I saw Joice from afar, I learned to be content with that glance. Each night, I twirled the jar and examined the squirrel wine and looked forward to consuming the coming potency.

揩

AS THE LEGAL HUSBAND, I went to the department of Justice to claim the Fake Wife. Gold Szeto's lawyer showed me her photo and told me again I had one chance at identification and then he would handle the rest. Do not answer any questions, he instructed as we got on the elevator. No problem, I said. We entered the large room. It was white and empty and there wasn't a chair or a table or a person, not even a secretary or a desk. What kind of official building was this? I wondered. We were all men, in the room there were only Chinese men. A guard entered the room.

We men congregated in front of a huge window, which looked into a dark room. A light switched on and the other side was illuminated and women started to file in and so I remembered my own arrival and my own waiting for my fake Father to identify me in the lineup and then likewise how I was asked to pick him out of a line of fathers.

I saw the Fake Wife easily. As agreed, she wore a blue

dress with yellow roses cascading down the front. The color combination had sounded unremarkable, but in the room of dark tunics, her dress was the sky and the beaded buds like a hundred suns. The number on the card she held by her hip identified her as Immigrant Number 55549. I copied it and handed that along with our marriage certificate to the lawyer who disappeared down the long corridor.

No one else was called from the room, so it felt like a long while of nothing happening, but when the door opened again, Ilin Cheung was delivered to me. The first thing I noticed was that hers was not a quiet prettiness, but the fiery sort that was Louie's preference, more mistress than wife. Her mouth had a firm set and her nostrils flared slightly, which gave her, even in repose, a fierce tigress look. Her eyes were wide set and her gaze direct.

Husband.

Her voice was low and had a smoker's density.

Wife.

As stiffly, we stood and waited. When the lawyer returned, he shook my hand and I understood the paperwork cleared, we were victorious. Then as instructed, I took her to Gold Szeto's. I waited outside his office and listened to one voice rising and another leveling until silence slipped out like a sheet of wind from underneath the door. She emerged, not looking upset or victorious, but satisfied, like she'd put up a good fight.

You all right? I asked.

She was sucking on her lower lip and I noticed a crescent-shaped scar, which gave her a petulant expression. Thirsty, she said.

I took her to Fong-Fong's Ice Creamery and ordered her a three-flavored sundae, thinking something new would distract her. One new discomfort to replace the other, I said.

Very yang, she said.

Perfect for your temper, I teased. Cooling.

She took a first bite of vanilla and then asked, Where's the cherry?

I called out to Fourth Fong and he brought a plate of them, which made her laugh. To my surprise, she ate all three scoops and then smiling, sank back into the booth.

What did he want, I asked.

Same as I want, she said.

And what's that? I asked.

Freedom, she said.

The Dream, I said.

I looked around the soda fountain. In the next booth, a little girl leaned over and admired Ilin's tall hairdo. The little girl said, You're pretty.

Ilin smiled and said, Girls in America aren't shy.

You'll get used to it all, I said. Everything must feel alien but beginnings are always hard. A few falls and it's nothing. Soon enough, you'll forget and the past will haunt less and less so that soon it will be a weak whistle from an abandoned tunnel. You'll stop going back to your past because it will lead to boredom, which is what all you can't change becomes. And then you'll crave the unfamiliarity you are afraid of now. I smiled. I was like you in the beginning. When I first arrived, I didn't have a dream to latch my mind onto. Trust me, one day everything that is unbearable will become as regular as an ice cream at four o'clock on a Wednesday. You may want to go back now, but one day you might refuse to go, might even fight it. Believe me, it's true, What you fear becomes what you must bear.

What are you talking about? she asked.

The trick is not to think too much. Life should be fun. This is the Flowery Kingdom!

I like fun, she said.

I'm sure you do, I said.

So why are you telling me this? She gestured for a cigarette.

I lit one for her and said, Maybe you remind me of someone I used to want to be.

She exhaled and said, I doubt it.

I'll give you some advice an old timer in the Square gave me: Accept no hand that promises protection. The bigger hand strikes with the hardest palm.

Did I say I was afraid? she asked.

No you didn't.

Maybe we will both need each other's hand at some point, she said.

You're probably too clever for me, I said.

A woman needs to be, don't you think?

Come on! I said. We have a few hours before the banquet so let's stop talking, let's have some fun! I borrowed Louie's car and took her for a drive through the Presidio to the Golden Gate Bridge, then out to Ocean Beach and the Sutro Baths. I drove to the Marina, showed her the yachts and sailboats on the calm bay and then wove back through Lombard to Mason. When I pulled into the last diagonal spot at the very top of the Broadway steps, she gasped.

So steep! she exclaimed.

We got out of the car and walked to the stone steps. I pointed to the Bay Bridge. This is the best view, I said. And this is the best seat.

Why, she asked.

Under a full moon, it's like being back home.

I'm never going back, she said. I came here for two reasons and one day, I will ask for your help in a matter.

I watched the cars inching across the Bay Bridge and

thought, Escape. I didn't dare mention my confession to her and I didn't want to know any intimate details about her life. But she started telling it anyway and there was no stopping her. She locked me in, talking without pause, barely breathing. What else could I do but let her talk herself through?

I WAS the daughter with the nomad heart. My father was a typesetter for the township newspaper. He had the three thousand characters required for simple newspaper reading and he tendered that knowledge through a quick triangle: mind to eye to agile hand. He had a narrow hand and knuckles that unhinged like bamboo. His thumb flexed faster than a bookkeeper's on an abacus and his last nail was longer than an opium smoker's. He had hand-eye harmony, he had speed; his was a special talent, he could read characters in reverse.

From one tray he picked out metal characters and dropped them cube by cube into a wooden tray. Metal hit wood like running sand. One ideogram stacked against another till line by line, cube by cube, they made a story and all the stories added up to a page and the page became a sheet wide enough to wrap a baby in and the sheets all piled thick enough to blanket a beggar.

My father twilled each legion line. From blankness rose the believable, the news of why, when and how. Pages like surrender flags. The ghost ink of babies, the caked comfort-dirt of beggars.

Every word was a disease, each story was a disaster. After he assembled the story onto the tray, he slipped the thick leather strap over his neck, snapped the metal hooks onto the two notches on his belt and lifted the tray up onto his forearms and starting walking, the weight pulling on his neck like a cangue, the walk through the dark corridor, like the convicted.

The machines beat like drums, the beat echoed in his heart. The heated metal had the acrid odor of burnt squid and the vapor stung his eyes. When the cylinders roared and rolled and clicked, when the gears drummed and echoed, a thundering filled the cavernous plant like a hundred monks chanting.

After he dipped the horsehair brush into ink, he ran it over the story tray. The metal niblets glistened through the page like teeth ready to bite. Sheet by sheet, he fed the large squares into the spinning cylinders. The white was sucked in and came spitting out the other end, long black tongues, wet and wagging with the gossip of the world.

He remade the world onto paper. The *New China News*.

But the Father wanted more. He wanted the new world. So he and his older brother set sail from South China for Mexico. The Flowery Kingdom was their destination. They crossed the desert on foot and at San Ysidro, they hopped a train, but the Father was shot.

She set fierce eyes on me as if to swear an oath. That's why I said yes to the marriage broker, why I will fulfill my promise to Gold Szeto.

I THOUGHT her heart was like a white fist. Clenched. Bloodless. She carried revenge like blood in her mouth. She sailed across the Pacific, that Ocean of Peace, to find the Uncle as if looking for the ideal lover. If her father had lived, would he have taught her that desire wasn't a road to knowledge, that love was never ideal, that yearning was not hope?

Life is not a kung fu novel, I said. What happens in a book is written, what happens in life is lived. Another day, I said, I might read yours.

Though I did not doubt her sorrow or her grief, I worried about anyone who led with a confession. Was her telling pain or play? Knowing her story fostered a responsibility I did not want. I hadn't known her for more than a few hours and already she was pulling me into a confidence I neither earned nor desired. Here was a person with nothing in hand, so loss or gain was in the same palm. I resolved not to tell her about my confession; I did not trust that she might not tell Gold Szeto.

I felt for her but I would not let her buy me with her sad story. Yet, the decent man must respect the story given to him. No matter how manipulative the telling, no matter how common the theme, each story was a gift worthy of a response.

When I wished her a good outcome, she looked surprised. Was my response unexpected? Was my sympathy unwelcome?

There was no time to think about it, only enough to change and arrive at Four Seas to greet our first guests.

昭

THE BANQUET. Gold Szeto used the banquet to announce the union between Jack and Ilin to his associates and to the community. Seeing the floor of round tables filled with envious men, he privately celebrated his coming immortality. Soon enough, everyone would be returning to the Four Seas to celebrate the birth of his son.

Gold Szeto spared no expense. The Johnny Walker at each table was black, not red. The menu included a braised goose besides the three birds: squab, chicken and duck. The shark's fin was thin as vermicelli and the sea cucumber was rich with crunch. There were scallops and tiger prawns as well as the two indulgences: oyster and lobster.

All his workers and business associates were invited and so were the fired and retired that congregated at the Square. As if the groom, Gold Szeto personally greeted guests, believing their cooperation would insure his success. When everyone was seated, he surveyed the banquet hall and saw a sea of hungry faces and malleable loyalties.

Attendance was an agreement. The story, like the menu, was set.

Placement told the story. On Gold Szeto's right, an empty chair represented his barren wife, and to his left sat his Replacement Wife. Jack sat farther right, as her legal husband. This banquet was not a celebration of the union, rather an announcement of Gold Szeto's intent.

If any man had commentary, Gold Szeto wanted it voiced where he could hear it. He kept his speech short. Happiness is limited. Each man deserved his share. Gold Szeto raised his glass and shouted out the traditional toast: A hundred years' happiness to the Bride and Groom!

Whether surprised at his brevity or brazenness, the entire hall was quiet for a moment and then in a roar, each guest raised up a glass, shouting, One Hundred! One Hundred Happy Springs! Sons and Grandsons!

Gold Szeto was pleased. Eating was a signature of silence. The unspoken was the home of truth. This was the truth they ate and the truth they were committed to speak. The official story was the first course served: *I went to the son's wedding banquet, I toasted their hundred-year happiness. I was a witness.*

Gold Szeto shook his clasped fist and shouted out, Serve the banquet!

The kitchen doors swung open and waiters streamed out with tureens of soup. The butchers were seated by the kitchen so that the swinging doors and the fast moving track of waiters would drown out their raucous commentary.

Master Cleaver tasted the shark fin soup and admired the clear broth. Top grade fin! he said.

Mankok poured scotch into his bowl and said, Top grade means top secret.

May Gold Szeto have many sons! Gorman said, ladling himself a second serving.

Grandsons! Mankok corrected.

Fat Gee from the soy factory craned his neck at the wedding table. Why is there an empty chair next to Gold Szeto?

You're too stupid to live! Master Cleaver scolded. Don't you understand anything? The empty chair is True Wife's big empty womb.

Fat Gee tittered, True Wife is not happy being so far away from Gold Szeto's jade stem.

Broken Stem! Mankok said.

The Replacement Wife is very pretty, Fat Gee observed.

Of course she's pretty, Mankok scoffed, she's young! If she's not pretty when young, when? When? Not when old! If you ask me, I don't trust the pretty ones; when beauty goes, they're all Mean Tigresses.

Fat Gee surveyed the banquet hall and asked, Is Bathhouse Girl here? I like how she looks.

I saw her throwing up in the park, Mankok said as he packed two firm mounds of rice into his bowl.

Maybe she ate something wrong, Fat Gee said.

Mankok winked. Maybe, she *has*.

Has happiness? Fat Gee asked.

The men laughed. The scotch circled the table again. Master Cleaver snapped up a black mushroom from the newly arrived dish.

Fat Gee continued, In my opinion, bride's beauty is more traditional.

This is a wedding banquet, not a beauty pageant, Master Cleaver scolded.

Bride is more expensive is the truth! Mankok said.

Bathhouse Girl has nice eyes, Fat Gee said.

You like leftovers, Trash man. Mankok sneered.

Her smile is so nice, Fat Gee sighed.

Upper or lower? Mankok asked.

The men threw back their heads. Master Cleaver slapped his thigh, roaring loudest. Lower! Lower!

See her mouth? Never saw one so big, said Mankok.

Fat Gee nodded. One bite, she can do.

Do you! Do you! The men clapped and chimed.

Gorman pointed at his own nose, Two big mouthfuls don't fit mine!

Mankok shouted, She wouldn't look at big old, fat old, stinky old you!

Don't be so cruel! Brother Gorman is sweet! He swept his arms out, Ask any lady here!

Your old bones wouldn't sweeten a pot of soup! Master Cleaver sneered.

You go die! Gorman shouted. The ladies love me.

Love your bald head! Love! The men roared.

The waiters were leaving the kitchen so quickly the electric doors never fully shut and there was a continuous buzzbuzz and the red-vested waiters fluttered by like hummingbirds. A plate of prawns was presented and a dozen chopsticks pinched and clipped into it. The two indulgences arrived. Between happy bites, the men exclaimed, Gold Szeto has a generous heart, Gold Szeto deserves happiness.

All talk stopped when Louie Yue walked by with a golden-haired woman on his arm.

His damn mother! said Mankok.

Nine generations back! Master Cleaver cursed.

Silence was the new rare dish. There was no more chewing, no more swallowing, no more slurping. After Louie passed, everyone leaned their heads toward the center of the table, See? See that playboy?

Touching a Devil girl!

No manners!

Disrespectful!

A quiet brewed like an herbal tonic, each man pondering his own loneliness. The last platter was served and the men looked hard at the round soft shape, sniffing the anise fragrance.

Gorman explored the dish with his chopsticks, found a wing and broke it off. Goose! He tasted it and smacked his lips. Very tender, he said.

Very generous. Fat Gee sucked on the fleshy web.

Secrets aren't cheap, Mankok said. That bride is Gold Szeto's, Jack is only the stand-in husband.

Their marriage is fake? Fat Gee scratched his head.

More fake than your teeth! Mankok yelled. Don't you see how Gold Szeto is looking at her, with his big tongue?

The men laughed.

Look! Fat Gee jumped up. See how Bride puts on her lipstick!

What's so special about that? Gorman turned to look.

Economy of movement, Fat Gee sighed. She twists once with her thumb and the lipstick is all up. Looks very nice, looks like she's shy about her beauty, that's very nice.

You don't know about Lipstick Kung fu? Gorman smiled.

Very lethal! Fat Gee nodded.

Mankok shouted, Look at how your cow-eyes roll back and forth, don't look so crazy, you! Banquet people should be beautiful.

I tell you, some women use all ten fingers, smear the hand and miss the lips, Fat Gee insisted.

Master Cleaver scolded, What's the matter with you? Talking about another man's wife at his wedding banquet!

Why yell so loud? Gorman asked, Mao Tse Tung can hear you.

Mao Tse Tung's busy ruining lives with his Hundred Flowers Campaign! Master Cleaver grumbled.

The men picked once more through the platters. Be careful, Mankok said as he poured the last of the scotch. We eat Gold Szeto's food, we eat his lie. Be ready to spit out Gold Szeto's truth when the INS comes around. If they want to know if he owns the Universal, we answer No. When they ask if he owns 850 Jackson, we answer No. When they ask about the gambling houses or his partnership with Jim Mulligan, we answer, we don't know.

No problem. No problem.

No. No. No.

We don't know, don't know.

Each man gave a final flick through the dishes and finding no more morsels, rested their chopsticks over their bowls. Arriving empty handed, they left so. Exiting, every man offered an open palm to the father, the son and the bride.

Saying goodbye to his guests, Gold Szeto was pleased. He accepted their thanks. He gripped each hand. He looked into each man's eyes and read their obedience: envy, fear and respect.

揝

WHEN ILIN FIRST MENTIONED wanting to work, I suggested she needed a friend and Louie introduced her to Pegeen—who, being Irish born, encouraged Ilin to be independent and do as she wished, so Ilin came to the Universal and confronted Gold Szeto on the selling floor during the busiest time of the day. There was a lot of yelling. Customers put down their baskets, stopped rubbing the hairy melons. We butcher-brothers pulled our heads into our collars when she demanded, I want the bloodiest work, I want to start at the butchery. We worried, none of us wanted an ill-tempered woman with a three-pound cleaver in our two-by-three-foot passageway.

But it was I who was assigned to train her. I didn't think Gold Szeto knew that I'd entered the Confession Program but I didn't want to invite attention by refusing his orders. So, after being my bride, Ilin became my disciple at the butchery. Six days a week, we worked together. It could have been funny if she weren't so earnest. She had no natural talent. She didn't inherit her father's hand-eye coordination. Her grasp was not firm, her thumb did not wrap the handle, so her palm was no seat from which she could mount her strength. I cringed watching her. She held the cleaver as if it were made of cardboard. When her knife made contact, it was not a whack clear through to the butcher block but a series of thumps as if she were chasing a rodent. Her blade glanced off the breastsplates, lodged halfway into the short ribs and split the crunchy skin from the roasted pig. Customers demanded refunds. There was nothing to say when they opened up their pink cones to show me a heap of meat, skin and bone shards.

I tried to teach her hand-eye exercises to toughen her grip and improve her aim but it didn't help. Once she missed the board completely and nicked the cleaver on the steel counter. Another time, she sliced her hand and blood flowed till I got my sawdust remedy and sprinkled it over the open wound.

Debt of blood. I told her, Academy fees.

The Butcher-brothers teased me: Dumb disciple damns the Master. When Gold Szeto assigned her to the "soft" chores, stacking bok choy, pricing canned goods, tallying invoices on the abacus, walking the selling floor, I observed her gift, her authoritative ease on the other side of the counter. She confronted shoplifters without embarrassing them, soothed women who fought over pomelos, caught teenagers stealing candy, guided old men toward the door. No one felt slighted, everyone always felt special. Her power was patience.

After closing, I went into the storage room and searched through boxes and found a smaller cleaver. I stayed late to sandpaper off the rust and then another night to sharpen the blade and a third, seasoning the knife edge over a gas flame till the steel shone. Then I carved a new handle out of a chunk of red wood and sanded it smooth to fit her grip. I wanted something to focus her eye before she threw the blade, so along the top center of the handle, I carved three holes. It took another week but I finally found the right stones in a pawnshop on upper Grant. When I embedded the red, yellow and green stones in a single line along the handle, it was ready.

I flicked the edge with my thumb and heard the thin warble and checked its sharpness by slicing through thick sheets of butcher paper. Then I slipped it between the entertainment section of the *Times* and carried it out onto the selling floor where Ilin was stacking dried abalone.

To make your job easier, I said.

She tested its fit by passing it from her left to right hand.

Feel good? I asked.

Perfect, she said. Then she waved it like a ribbon dancer waving her strips of silk.

Careful, I said.

Smiling, she touched each stone and said, Just like traffic lights.

To steady your eye, I told her.

At the deli counter, I pulled the biggest bird off the rack and laid it on the chopping block. Endeavor, I said. Aim through bird, aim toward spine and stem, aim toward wood.

She tapped blade to bird. She took in a big breath. She threw her cleaver back. She slammed through to wood.

I was pleased; I taught her well.

At closing, I complimented her improved skills, which only stirred her to talk about her ultimate goals. So while we were cleaning the butchery, she continued her story:

Listen. Like anybody, I believed that what I didn't have

was what I most wanted. Without a father, I had no claim to a history and I felt beneath other people. I wanted a father's protection. When my mother mourned that there was no son to avenge his death, my grief doubled. Why was it that a son could offer blood but a daughter could only offer tears? Why was a daughter a spiritual orphan? Why did a daughter float between natal and marital families?

I set sail with the seven metals in my heart. I would find my Uncle. I would ask him why he'd forsaken his own brother. I believed action was the supreme retribution of feeling and all they felt would be retold in my deed.

WAIT, I INTERRUPTED. I made this cleaver for you so that you can do your job better.

I know that, she said.

I ventured, Do you really think like this?

Like what?

Are you really so unforgiving?

She turned away so I knew I caught her truth. I'm going to tell you one thing, I said and then I won't ever mention it again. We began as strangers but now we have a history, this is fact. As a friend, I ask you this: Do you really think you can be a better person after this confrontation? Isn't it better to live the life your father would have wanted you to enjoy?

Her look was as dull as the unseasoned blade.

I said, Don't pull me down with your strange ideas. Don't seduce yourself into thinking you can function in that kind of old world vacuum.

She looked at me like I was speaking a foreign language. Then she lifted the cleaver and flipped it over, once and then again, as if weighing her own words. Finally she said, He owes me, he owes in the memory of his brother.

He knows the laws of retribution and he expects me; if not in this life, in the next.

I shook my head and said, I'm telling you, I won't help you with that. You won't win in that sort of endeavor.

Miss? A customer interrupted. Can I order?

Her eyes narrowed beyond the customer to some distant point. She turned back to me and said, I don't look to win. With one hand, she slapped at her apron like a Minister uncuffed his sleeves before prostrating to the Emperor. Then, with the cleaver still in her other hand, she walked out from behind the deli counter onto the floor of the Universal.

I watched her and I worried.

昭

THE NEIGHBORS ON Wayne Alley were not on
Gold Szeto's payroll, so under his orders, I left a
change of clothes and stopped by every night. If nosey
Mrs. Lam was questioned by the INS, she could talk about
my cohabitation with Ilin as a true story.

Life was time and our time made love. From the ten
hours at the butchery to the nights on Wayne Alley, Ilin
and I built a friendship from time spent and it was natural
law that time stored up feelings like gold. After dinner at
Great Eastern and a drink at the Buddha, I visited Ilin. It
was late enough to give the neighbors the right impression. If Ilin was asleep, I'd read the paper and then leave.
Often, we had tea and visited.

She was still bored, she told me. Even more so since she
had to visit Gold Szeto's on Sundays and they had to do it.

It's hopeless, she said. My body will never have happiness.

One spring night, she welcomed me with an herbal
tonic.

It's special, she told me, her mother's last gift. Fifty-year-old ginseng, extremely potent.

I took the bowl and drank the bitterness in one swallow. The quiet was long and thin as a horn. She leaned in close and stroked my thigh and said, How do we handle this?

About? I put my hand over hers.

About us, she nodded. About us doing love.

What are you asking?

She looked straight into my eyes. Her eyes were still. I need to secure my position, she said. Gold Szeto wants a son.

I looked at her and said, If we walk this road, Gold Szeto may turn on you, turn on me. Are you prepared to face this?

She put her hand on me and whispered, Who wouldn't favor young to old?

When I felt the cup her hand made, I imagined her moist heat. You are not deaf or blind going in, I said. Gold Szeto is the fisherman and we are his cormorants.

Are you talking about that bird that works for very small reward? she asked.

I nodded. Gold Szeto has a ring around my neck, I fly to catch his fish, but I'm forbidden from swallowing my pleasure. I am not the Immortal Bird.

What bird? she wanted to know.

The one with the broken leg, doomed to fly forever because in flight it is free.

She stroked me. You know a lot of stories don't you?

Maybe I'm trying to make a new story for myself, I said. Wouldn't you prefer to live in another story?

Some stories are better than life. But you and I are caged in this one, she said.

Her eyes were as luminous as a lake in moonlight.

I wanted to believe her. I wanted to believe something bound us, that mutual need made us equals. But whose need was larger? So I kissed her to test my own resolve.

You and I, she kissed back and said, We are the same, we are alone in the world.

And so we did fly. Our legs were broken. Our surrender was to land.

To ascend the bed.

That was one term, the one we used.

Another term, To do love.

Her hands were softer than breath and her breath was sweet, more languid than black poppies. The whole of me was lost. I felt a cooling like a strand of pearls and then that razor snap of the necklace breaking. Her intent was in her breath, complete and filling and I was back in the safe hold of the river-mother.

We mounted the bed.

We did love.

Which was the original?

Which the translation?

智

WHEN EDSO SAID Louie left word that he needed to talk, I left the café right away and headed for the Buddha. My first step into the bar, I knew there would be trouble, it was too smoky and there was a sugary aroma, as if too many tourist drinks had been spilled. Our usual opera wasn't playing, but a drumbeat like a headache pounded out from the jukebox. At the center of the horse-shoe bar, two men were laughing too loud, their eyes darting back and forth like knives sharpening.

I found Louie at the end of the bar and gestured back at the strangers. Who are they?

Foot cops, Louie said. From the Vallejo precinct.

Winston poured us scotch and said, They could be from Sansome Street, they could be INS.

Edso gave me your message, I said to Louis, What's going on?

He said, Let's leave. Then a distressed woman cried out from the back, Just you try! I turned and saw a large man by the phone booth and a blond woman pushing away from him. I recognized the Messenger and said, Brother, We meet again.

He acknowledged me the way a man who had not yet fought did.

It appears the woman doesn't want to talk to you, I said.

Get out of my way, he said and rushed past.

A whistle came from the center of the bar. Come back, come back Baby. We're your kind.

Leave her alone, Louie said.

Both cops were watching. The larger one got off his stool, walked up to Louie and demanded, Don't you live on Vallejo?

Louie answered in English, What business is that of yours?

You the Chinaman living with our Pegeen McShane?

Louie stood up to him.

You should stay with your own, Large Cop said.

I said to Louie in Cantonese, Don't get involved.

Speak English! Small Cop yelled, You're in America.

We know that, Louie countered in English.

The cops started singing, but something was not right, the melody was common but something about it barely survived translation. But it wasn't till they hit the chorus that I knew it was a bastardization of our "Flower Drum Ballad."

Louie demanded, Why you sing that?

You like? Small Cop jeered and Large Cop joined in.

The beat got simple, the beat got stupid, there was no mistake.

Louie stood up and said, Someone better get me out of here.

I heard his tightness and said, Let's go over to Lambert's Club.

Louie went up to Large Cop, You like that song?

Large Cop cocked his head back. He sang out, Me li-kee, you likee?

Louie gave me a quick nod and I knew the code in his flat look, the coming explosion of fire, so I took in my reserve-breath.

Louie yelled, Eat Shit!

I saw Louie's arm punch Large Cop's face. I saw Small Cop's hand reach into his jacket and I yelled, At-tend, left!

Louie rammed into him and shouted, Let's get out!

We ran out of the Buddha, up Jackson, all the way to the cable car barn. Then we cut through Himmelman Place, Salmon Alley and out onto the top of Broadway. At the stone bench, I looked down the hundred and thirty-nine stone steps, following the carpet of lights all the way to the Bay Bridge.

Louie pointed at the two figures crossing lower Broad-way, heading toward Fiorelli's lot and shouted, Let's go!

We ran to Taylor and then down onto Joice, snaking through the garden path back into Chinatown. On Vallejo, the police station was lit, a lone firefly on the dark residential street. Louie spit on the windshield of the cruiser-cop car. Laughing, we ran past Victoria's Pastry on Stockton, Rossi's Market on Kearney. All was dark, all was locked up. Only St. John's Cathedral on the corner glowed white. Caffe Trieste was open and Long-Hairs were smoking in the street, their music like snakes slipping out of a safe crevice.

We crossed Upper Grant, climbed up the hill to Louie's place. As soon as we walked in, a voice rolled down the hallway. Sweetheart?

As Louie spoke to Pegeen, I saw a stance and heard a tone of a different man. To give them privacy, I listened to the warmth above the words, glanced away from their curving intimacy.

Then I glimpsed a shimmering, a sweeping motion like a bird in flight.

Honey? Pegeen's voice came again.

I looked down the long corridor and saw a line of doors like boxcars on a freight train. Then I saw Pegeen. Her belly glowed, a globe like an immortal pearl rising. Then I remembered seeing Joice leaving Sam Wo's earlier in the week and how I was startled at her body's new form.

Go back to bed, Louie's smooth voice was firm. Go rest.

Then he motioned for me to follow. I smelled roses as I passed them on the narrow hallway. Standing in the dark kitchen, I noticed there was no ginger scent, no lingering spice, no aroma of meals shared. Louie came and unlocked the kitchen door and I followed him up the back stairs to the roof, where we found the door padlocked. He kicked it but it didn't give. I shouted, Again!

We pushed back from the wall and rammed the door. It punched out and we fell onto the gravel roof, laughing. Louie rolled up against the ledge. I stood in the darkness, feeling the inside of my chest beating as if there were a thousand swallows in flight. Louie's face was gambler-calm but I saw that the tendon along his neck bulged like a finger.

I pointed at the ring around the moon and said, Rain tomorrow.

Then those two cats won't be doing foot duty, Louie said.

I can't afford to get into trouble; I worried out loud.

Trouble finds us, Louie said.

Is there anything you're afraid of? I asked.

That's why I want your help. I need to register the new baby with my name.

Why don't you give the doctor some tea money? I suggested.

I did, only to have him warn me not to try that again.

Maybe your bribe was too little? I teased.

He laughed, Don't try bribing a Bamboo born-here doctor, they're not loyal to their own blood. Brother, he said, I want a favor.

Of course, I said.

Ask Gold Szeto to help me.

I got up and leaned over the tar ledge, the streets below were as black and as empty as the inside of oil barrels. A blue car slipped like grease into a parking space. I'll wait for the opportunity, I said. It's hard to catch him in a generous mood. Then I asked, Aren't you afraid someone will send word back to your wife about this baby?

Louie shrugged. Let's see if it's a son first.

I shook a finger at him. If you favor boy over girl now, don't cry when your child is disfavored for being mixed blood.

He stood and drew his fist back and punched at the darkness. I can't worry about that. I have to enjoy myself before the Mean Tigress emigrates!

I want to know, Which woman is dearer to your heart?

Louie's hesitation spoke his pain. His silence was not indecision, rather it was as if he was the new sort of man, where straddling two worlds was a doubling of love.

Pegeen understands my *heart-thinking*. Then he sighed, as if defeated. But Yuenling is Chinese, and in the end, the ancestors must be honored.

In the distance, the foghorns blew and I imagined the ocean renamed Great Calm, a boat called Escape.

Women! Louie said, They can ruin with a smile. I started up with Pegeen because her smile made me feel free. Her hair like fire, skin like water, everything about her made my senses dance.

She's lit you up, Brother.

Louie smiled, Pegeen's ruthless though. The woman who has her heart set on you will never let go. The simpler the woman, the more tenacious her grip.

I'm a working man, I said. I can't afford a woman with an extravagant temper.

Don't die one, Louie said. That's my advice to you. Find your happiness and enjoy it. Don't save it up, it won't keep. Joy vaporizes unless you worship it.

When I asked how he was going to explain this baby to his wife in China, he got upset. Why should I explain my life? I slaved and sent her all my sweat-money, for what? Only to eat her letters of grief. Only this much? Why? Are you gambling and whoring while your wife and old mother eat tree bark? Louie grabbed a fistful of gravel and threw it over the roof. The sound like rain, like tears.

He continued, What do women know about our suffering? Have you ever counted the words that have kept you a coolie? The Flowery Kingdom has only one word for us: No. No to you. No to Mankok Fong. No to Gorman Ginn. No. Louie continued, And from back home, the word *Should* hangs around our necks like a cangue. *Should. Should* work harder. *Should* work more. *Should* send more money home. *Should! Should! Should!*

Why get so upset? I asked.

Why aren't you? he asked. You should be too, he said. Obligation and loyalty has no accounting in Gold Szeto's book. You've already paid him back. His compassion wouldn't fill a teacup. Brother! My advice to you is this: Be a merchant of the heart! As if to punctuate his declaration, Louie threw another fistful of stones over the roof.

I listened to the stones bouncing from fire escape to fire escape and then scattering over the tops of the garbage cans on the street. I knew Louie was talking about himself. Talking to me was only a way to hear his own answers. Brother, I said, Don't borrow my problems as a platform to bemoan yours! I'm not like you. One, I need a family and two, I need to work.

Family. Work. Louie said the words as if they were a disease.

These two words held the worlds I wanted to inhabit. Would I be fulfilled through family and work? What about love? Would I dare wish for both? There was no breeze and this late, there was not even a human sound. I looked out into the dark city and felt a thundering in my ears; I was hearing my blood beating toward its source. Soon my heart would be my only true sensation. No breath, just pulse. I got up and walked across to the opposite edge, welcoming the new sound of gravel crunching like cicadas beneath my feet. I watched the headlights blinking across the bridge and felt a new road opening before me.

What else is going on? Louie asked.

Louie's question caught me off guard.

There's something else with you tonight, he said.

I paused, not because I didn't trust Louie to keep this secret, but because I didn't trust myself, what was it I felt? Had I given up on Joice? Had I accepted that Joice had given up on me? I was asking my friend for an interpretation.

Ilin and I, we *ascended* the bed.

Louie smiled, Normally I would encourage this cloud-play, but as your brother, I advise caution. I'm not saying she's a bad person, but she holds the power because she can give Gold Szeto a blood son. You're aware of this, aren't you?

She told me herself, I nodded.

So don't be blind going in, Louie said.

How do I protect myself? I asked.

Forget it, Louie said. In the Flowery Kingdom, there's no protection! Women hold the power; women and white men.

What's the hope then? I wanted to know.

Louie smiled, What else? I hope to have fun.

潛

ONE DAY TO clean one hundred thousand. Gold Szeto spent ten days in Hong Kong. Upon return, we didn't see him for another ten days, that's how long it took to reset the funds back into a new gambling house on Bayshore. But at the Universal, we were always ready for his arrival. When he finally showed up, it was opening time and he walked with the Messenger through the entire market. He surveyed the dry good aisles and checked the fruit and vegetable displays. He walked so slowly by the stacks of Dungeness crab and sea bass and rock cod, I thought he was counting them, but I saw he was checking the eyes. At the deli counter, he pointed at a duck and said, Pluck it clean!

At the butchery, he looked into the meat display cases. But when I greeted him, he walked on without reply. Throughout the rest of the day, he seemed to purposely ignore me.

When I mentioned his demeanor to Ilin, she said not to worry.

I'm still anxious, I said.

She looked at me a long while and then said, There's something going on with you tonight.

I drew a breath and then said, My daughter was born today.

That's good news, isn't it? A daughter is wonderful.

Her excitement gave me courage and I told her. Today, Joice gave birth at Chinese Hospital. Old Lady Qwan came to tell me the good news, I had a daughter, and then the not-so-good news, Joice didn't care to see me. After work, I went there anyway and had the good luck to run into Cookie Wing who was visiting her sister. Candy was head nurse on the third floor and she took me to the nursery and I was overwhelmed. There must have been at least fifty babies. Swaddled in white blankets and caps, the nursery looked like rows and rows of fresh dumplings. Candy walked down the narrow aisles, checking wrist tags. From behind the glass, I saw eyes squeezed tight as guppies. I held my breath when she picked up a baby and carried her to the window. Asleep, the baby's lashes rested on her cheeks like points of a star. I took in a deep breath and just watched her. When her fist pushed upward and her tiny mouth opened and she yawned, I was tremulous with feeling.

Is she pretty? Ilin asked.

What? I didn't know how to answer that. She's still small, I said.

Ilin shook her head and said, I'm sorry. I wasn't thinking, I was just repeating what people back home say when a girl is born. But this is the new world, and prettiness is not a promise of a daughter's future, as sons are not a guaranteed blessing.

That's right, I said.

Have you named her?

No one asked me, I said.

She stroked my hand, Don't think about the sad. Be happy, you're a father.

The quiet was voluminous as a conch shell. When she got up and walked across the room, I was mesmerized. She was wearing that blue dress I first saw her in and the curve from her neck down her long back rippled like water. I watched her uncork the brandy and pour a shot. When she glanced back at me, her eyes were shimmering. She drank one in a swallow and then poured two more and came gliding back toward me, her blueness more fluid than before. In front of me, she was a column, a waterfall, a flow of eternity.

She kept her eyes on me.

What do you want? I asked.

She had another shot. Then she handed me mine and without taking her eyes off me, lowered herself onto my lap. I drank it and then reached around and stroked her smooth back. She leaned in close. Her wide forehead was as innocent and wonderful as a newborn's.

You are sweet, I said.

A long slow smile filled her.

Yes? I asked.

I thank you, she said.

I felt her warmth and touched her.

My body has happiness, she said.

Then she put my hand on her belly.

She smiled, I want this child to be a son.

After a day of circular talking, I had no more words, so I lifted her and carried her into the bedroom. I undressed her and kissed her and then I drank her in. My thirst and her insatiability made us fearless. The final time, she cried out so fiercely I lifted up and said, Is there a fire?

Then we laughed and laughed and after, just lay there

catching our lost breath. The curtains were open, first I felt the breeze slipping in and then I smelled the tea of moisture and brine. Ilin said she was hungry and so we got dressed and went down to Sam Wo's and ordered up congee and her favorite midnight noodles.

Ilin had happiness.

We made more happiness. For weeks, we consumed happiness. I craved her touch and I devoured her. I let our sex extinguish my fear of remembering all I had hoped for with Joice. As time passed and as my hand explored the beginning swell of Ilin's belly and as I felt a rising that was like a grave mound, I ached imagining another life. Then I let the sex give me the daring to hope that I would soon hold my daughter.

This was my passage. As I grew to crave every change in Ilin's body, a sadness also grew inside of me. My desire for Ilin was not like my ache for Joice. With Ilin, we had a defined road. With Ilin, we had a camaraderie. So I touched and touched as deep as I could reach and Ilin was not naïve. She let me, and she let me.

One night, an image woke me. I was standing in the long corridor of Louie's apartment. I saw Pegeen again; I saw that glow in the rise of her belly. I smelled the crisp jasmine scent and I heard her honeyed voice calling to Louie and his gentle urge she return to bed. And then I was again embracing Joice in the narrow corridor of Old Spanish Alley. I woke in a sweat. Which road was darker, which was longer? Which was safe?

Loving had never been peaceful with Joice. She and I were orphans—without care, without purpose, without love and without devotion—our only concern was with the sun rising and the sun setting. I still yearned for her voraciousness, still ached for her greed, her declaration of surrender and the abyss of aloneness she worshipped. But all that was gone and all I could do was imagine her body, alone in the glow of magnificence after giving life. What was Joice feeling after birthing? How did my daughter resemble me? These imaginings shook me.

We believed life began at conception. Veda's first month was celebrated with a haircut and red eggs and she was considered one year old. I cried with joy for this tiny being arriving like dew.

昭

I TOLD LOUIE, if there was a chance of Gold Szeto's generosity, it would come after opening time at the Universal, but that chaotic Saturday, we were not lucky. I was at the take-out deli, helping set up when there was a loud knock and I opened the door. Baker Chan shoved in with his stacks of boxed cakes on a dolly. Right behind, Lee from Lee's Grocer pushed in with his wooden vegetable crates. Then the Fishmonger rolled in with a huge pail of fish. They collided. Lee's hand truck overturned and the vegetable crates fell and crushed Chan's cakes. Water spilled from the fish pails. Gorman couldn't see behind the large suckling pig he was wheeling and crashed his roasted pig into the chaos.

Wow all your mothers! Gorman cursed, picking up two pieces of his pig cheek.

The worst damage was that the skin of the roasted pig cracked.

Your mother! Lee thrust out his chin like a weapon, Whose butthole?

Yours! Gorman shouted.

There was a sound and I turned to see Ilin scraping her two raised cleavers like an assassin.

You all want a major incident with Gold Szeto? Ilin's voice had the *ving!* of the two knives crossing.

Like tortoises, Gorman and Lee drew their necks back in, coughing up apologies. Lee restacked his tower of vegetable crates and wheeled them to the refrigerators and then dragged his cart out, leaving the double doors open. I started to go lock them but Mankok was having trouble with the barbecue trays and helped him, I hung the ribs and the strips of BBQ pork. Then I arranged the skewers of chicken hearts, gizzards and the petal bunches of livers and after that, I lined the birds by size and color, chickens then ducks then quails, the roasted squabs last. The rule was dark to light in color and flavor: salt-baked then anise spiced, dark soy then pale-boiled. Just as I finished spearing the sparrows and chicken wings and stood them like armament across the window ledge, Gorman brought up the prepared foods. We dropped the trays into the heating table: chicken feet and pig ears: sautéed three style mushrooms, braised tofu, stewed tripe, beef with peppers, clams with black beans, innards and blood pudding, and large bulbous octopus, floating like bright pink lanterns. Then came the hardest task. Gorman and I used a two-by-four to hoist the suckling pig up to the deli window. We had to lift it several times, angling the pig face to hide the cracked cheek, so that fortune would smile upon us all.

At a quarter to eight, Gold Szeto stepped out onto the mezzanine for a few minutes, governing all with one sly glance. We had learned the eye-vocabulary of his displeasure, a long narrow glance at a melon stack-up meant wrong height. The downturned lip was for the wrongly positioned fish head or the unlucky number of winter gourds. A grunt was general ill humor. But today, all seemed in order and in harmony. Gold Szeto accepted our collective greeting and walked back into his office. We went back to our stations, feeling like chosen subjects, at play as a fake family.

I didn't know what to think when I opened the Universal doors and collided with the five men. I didn't have time to question them. They charged past me and threw a thick envelope onto the counter; they had no weapons but silver badges and a harsh brand of English. Three of them shouted and spread to triangle points on the ground floor, herding all of us into the center. Two ran up the stairs to the mezzanine.

AFTER.

Everyone stood with their mouth open as the front doors swung shut after Gold Szeto was escorted out. We shook our heads in disbelief. We stared at the door, not knowing if we should follow our boss out or lock ourselves in. We mumbled our sympathies to the forgotten man.

No one said the word Deport.

AS I WATCHED the suited men push Gold Szeto out of the Universal, I saw that his fists were clenched beyond the handcuffs. He turned once and cursed, I will be repaid! That was his last decree. But I couldn't be sure whom he was directing this to. I stared at his straight hard back as he left the Universal. That was my last view of the man I called Father.

No one moved as if we were locked inside the storage refrigerator. No one spoke as if for fear of lost air. Never had it been so still at the Universal.

From the butchery, I caught Ilin's harsh eyes. My guilt was already settling into me but with her fierce look, my fear doubled.

Ilin raised her cleaver and her voice, This isn't a movie, business is business! Open the doors!

THE WARRANT

Q: What is your name?
A: Yi-Tung Szeto

You are served with warrant of arrest, ordered by Judge Richard D. Smith, charging that you are an alien person unlawfully within the United States, in that you entered without inspection under the Immigration law Section 20, and in it that you entered in violation of another ("any") law of the United States, to wit, the Chinese Exclusion Laws, Section 21 of the Act of February 20, 1907. Can you furnish any evidence that you are not guilty of this charge, either by documentary evidence or by witnesses?

NO

If you say that, then it must be true.
I don't know a Jim Mulligan.
I don't own any property. The law forbids it, you know that.

I never sold gin. There was prohibition.
I don't know about any gambling house on Bayshore.
I have one wife. She is in China.

NO

Leave it as it is.
I don't remember it.
I don't want to read it.
I don't want it read to me.
I don't know how to sign that.
I don't want to sign it.
I don't have relatives.
I don't know.

NO

I forgot.
I don't care.
I don't remember.
You asked me that before.
If you are not satisfied with my statement, I can't help you.

NO

There is no use asking me any more questions.
I have nothing to report.
Do what you want.
Send me back to China.
It's no problem for me.

NO

II

respond

the handshake

EVEN THOUGH the government managed to seize the stock and inventory at the import emporium, it was Jim Mulligan's name on the deed and so there was no proven connection with Gold Szeto. Since Brothers Two and Three held the promissory notes on the property, business continued at the Universal.

When Gold Szeto sent word for his possessions to be shipped, he wanted it done by Jack. It took him about a week to pack the personal effects and the last thing left was to crate the camphor desk. The night the shippers were due, Jack stayed late to finish the job. In the basement, he slipped the ceramic pedestals into the wooden crates, packed the sides with straw and nailed on the covers. It took several packing blankets and a whole roll of twine to wrap the length of camphor securely and when he leaned it against the wall, the padded cylinder shape reminded him of the hanging coffins he had seen along the river cliffs. Then he heard the front door opening, assumed it was the shippers and headed up the stairs. Two quick shadows slipped in, as quiet as if entering a temple.

He felt the stillness of their shut heart, he felt the chill of their brute intent.

Did Jack know? Did Jack feel?

The shorter one was ox-slow and as strong, he lifted the wooden chair as if it was made of straw and placed it by the meat mincer.

Sit, the taller man ordered.

The voice was familiar but it wasn't till Jack saw the man's scarred lip that he recognized the Messenger.

Jack greeted him, Brother.

We have business, the Messenger said.

One day adversary, another day kin.

Jack searched for a needle of vertical light in the stone eyes but it was as if he was looking into the flat secret side of a two-way mirror. He read a face more rigid than a tombstone dog. What do you want, he asked.

If nimble, if bold. Foot and brow. Nine hearted. Empty-faced.

Suddenly, the men lunged at him, their arms and legs mirroring, equal shift of weight, equal force of fists. Jack fought to rise but they shoved him back down. The ice light flickered on and he felt the whiteness like a sheath. The Messenger leaned in, poured his molten words into Jack's ears: Gold Szeto does not forget.

Jack collected his shallow and middle breath in reserve, as he did before going into the airless freezer. His lungs expanded, filling up. He stored life deep within, safely cold. He felt each sensation slowing as if being preserved under prayer oil. When he heard heavy footsteps moving away, he knew it was the unsteady gait of a man who favored intoxicants. The lock bolted once, and then again, revolutions into the forever. Then they rushed at him and he felt a sack swallowing his head. They kicked at his ankles and straightened his limbs along wood. Jack felt his liver jamming up against the chair; he felt thick ropes binding him. Just a few moments ago, he had held his own knives and he could still feel the grit of the stone slab scrubbing against his palm, the tissue layer of moisture like a salve.

Tell me! he demanded, What do you want?

They punched hemp into his mouth and it felt as if his words were being stuffed down into his throat. He retched and then pitched forward, his forehead hitting the ground, a fake prostration.

A click, an earring of sound.

He heard it and knew. The band saw. The buzzing was low and smooth and then it quickly rose to a high pitch. He heard the hum of the overhead lights, he felt the vibration like the rubbing of insect legs along his brow and he heard sounds slipping in from the street: a bus hissing, heels on the pavement, a man's murmur.

He struggled to open his mouth but the hemp sunk in further. Then he was pulled up by his collar and his legs were dragged up into the butchering station. His heartbeat stilled.

A mouth lowered, hot breath beat the words into his ear, Be still. If you value your daughter. If you want to protect her.

His head jerked toward the voice, but there was no time to rename or negotiate.

JACK'S HEART SWAM back to the memory of his mother taking him across the river. He remembered slipping his hand into hers, hands soft as river water and as cool. The boat moved downriver chasing northern light, they were heading toward a big rock that rose out of the river like a fist. Three characters were painted on the rock and when his mother read them out, her voice wavered.

Toward

I

Come.

Trust rock, she told him. Empty your heart, she taught him. Break fear upon rock. Like the river masters, surrender to nature. Go toward fear. Trust fear. Steer toward rock.

The Mother.

Jack's heart returned to rest on the memory of love. He filled himself up with the roar of water, the rise of rock. This was a blood debt and maybe he owed it. Better he make the payment than his daughter. The taste of blood bit the back of his throat like salt on a raw wound. After the first swallow, he knew, he would have no fear.

Now his mother's voice rose in him like a rush of wings: *The empty heart had no mourners.*

He steered toward danger, he trusted the river-mother.

JACK MOON SZETO! Today is your payment day. Prepare yourself! The Messenger's voice was as composed as if he were drinking tea in the parlor. He said, Gold Szeto sends you this greeting. Life in the Motherland is good.

Jack's hand was gripped in a handshake.

Then he felt the cool chrome on his forearm. He felt the whir of the blade and then there was a dryness, a powdering mist. He counted the pegs of time clicking forward. How long was each revolution? He felt the many arms of a struggling Buddha. He felt the metal chewing through cartilage, slicing through bone.

The emptying, Noooooooo.

The calm, the filling, the eternal.
Stop!

But the temple bowl was cracked. Metal would not rim with song and no cry would release his body. How far to fly? Which land, which shore? Where was safety?

The Dead Past.

The Fixed Future.

This Ever Present.

JACK ONLY REMEMBERED the last impression of a handshake. In the stillness, he was confused between what was new and what was old.

Which hand did they shake?
Which hand did they take?

eternity 1

HAPPINESS.

I wasn't happy when I came to my new village. Every night, I waited till the house murmured with sleep and then I rolled up my mat and stole down the long lane to the Common House, where old men and orphan boys slept. An Old Traveler and his foreign wife had built it for the village. He was so lonely after she died, he moved to the Common House in her memory.

The Old Traveler's name for me was Little Friend. One night, he gave me a gift. I unwrapped the sheets of a foreign newspaper and found a lotus bean cake. When I bit through the flaky crust, the bean paste crumbled over my tongue like new soil.

THE OLD TRAVELER TOLD ME: *The heart never travels.*

It became my rule and ritual constant. What I knew, I kept in my four chambers. I kept my heart still as a fist.

Telling bound; telling deepened aloneness. I never

wanted my daughter bound to my history so I will never tell it to her. This was honoring ritual. It was forgetting not forgiving that completed repayment.

Released, I returned.

THE OLD TRAVELER TOLD ME: What you know, you will own forever. Some secrets are better left untold, some stories have been lived beyond telling. For optimum health, consume only seven parts out of ten. In eating, always leave a morsel. In sorrow, leave one memory sacred. In anger, leave one step untaken so that the other may descend the stage. In love, leave one word unspoken. In telling any story, exercise caution. An uttered word is not wind but bone.

I carried the Old Traveler's teaching across the Great Ocean of Peace into the Flowery Kingdom and I hope to give it to my daughter before I enter the Netherworld.

III

requite

報応

坦白

MY STORY WAS news and compassion was high and I could not afford to be prideful. My livelihood was lost and butchering was no longer an option. So when old bosses came forward with offers, I accepted. At Chong's Laundry, I worked the front desk, marking packages, recording pickups, and doing the late deliveries; it felt like boy's work but I did not complain. Then Old Chong lost his lease, so I cashiered at Ho Wan 56 for the winter, and in the spring, I was the broth man at Mayflower Noodles. Finally, all of it didn't suit me, it felt like woman's work, so I signed up with On Sang Employment Agency. Every week, I slipped tea money to the receptionist in order to get the best placements, but every week there was a new girl.

They sent me to several eateries before I settled for my longest period of employment at Ocean Palace, where I deep-fried wonton, drumsticks and spring rolls before moving to the roasting hut. I was good with fire, I knew just when to flip the ribs to burn the fat to a crispy char.

I knew how to snap and turn the suckling pig in order to singe off the hairs and roast the skin to a crispy pucker. I knew by smell how much hoisin and honey caramelized a duck's skin to a lacquer sheen. I was the Roasting King of Chinatown and I felt I'd found a place to begin again. But my reprieve was short-lived. After Hong Kong investors bought the restaurant, the new management started firing the old crew. When the Slick Hair Jue handed me a week's pay in cash, I threw the white envelope back at him and headed out. As I passed the roasting station, I felt the heat and kicked the plate glass hard enough to crack it.

For what? Louie asked when I stopped in at the Buddha. You only ruined yourself, he said. Chinatown is different now, he said. Look at the employment lines outside of On Sang, they're filled with men who work for even cheaper wages than our generation. It used to be that one job lasted a lifetime. Now, the job served the life.

Louie was negotiating to buy the Buddha Bar and wanted me to partner with him but I'd learned not to mix blood with business and so I chose friendship. A few weeks later, when I heard that Old Herbalist Woo was returning to the Motherland, I visited and asked if his stall was for sale.

Old Woo glanced at my empty sleeve and said, Stock and lease, five hundred is fair. You have a young daughter.

That night, I went down to the Square to think about it. But I walked into the Harvest Moon carnival. Even after nine, the park was filled with families, teenagers and tourists. Music blared, colored lights blinked above the concession stands and the whole park smelled like burnt sugar and rancid oil. The ground was sticky from spilled drinks, spun candy and peanut shells. I circled the park twice before finding a seat by the water fountain. Then I watched girls with porcelain shoulders climbing into teacups as wide as chairs. Boys followed them, tossing gum wrappers at their feet. When the ride started, the chairs started to twirl and the girls' heads percolated up like boiling water but the boys' heads stayed still as flat water.

I sat and watched and enjoyed the colorful distraction. I felt a generator rumbling underneath and I looked up toward the Ferris Wheel. Somehow I wasn't surprised to see Joice in a carriage, her legs dangling over the bars like a cricket's. The ride was unloading and as her carriage descended, the moon's muted light softened the lines of her face. I wondered what she was doing here alone and I walked over to meet her. She got off the carriage and we moved through the crowds, the quiet slipping between us like lint. We stopped at the water fountain and watched people walking into the Spinner, a ride with cages that lined the outer rim of a giant disk.

Did you work the late shift? I asked.

She nodded.

How's Veda? I asked. What is she learning?

She laughs like you, Joice said.

I watched a worker locking the riders into the cages, the huge disk lifting till it was perpendicular to the platform. You were right about Gold Szeto, she said.

We both didn't say anything for a while. Then Joice asked, What are your plans?

Suddenly the pink and silver lights started flashing and the disk started spinning, the different colors of each cage swirled together into a single rainbow and I thought my life was as thrown-about, I felt locked into a cage and spun by events I had no control over. The large twirling disk hypnotized me and even when it cranked to a stop, even after the cage doors opened and the riders tumbled out like laundry, I still felt compelled to keep my eye on it.

I don't know yet, I said. And I didn't know why I didn't tell her about the tonic stall.

Jack?

Yes? When I turned to her, she looked softer than I'd ever seen, but her stillness scared me. A crowd of kids walked by and their innocent laughter made me even sadder.

Peace, all right? Joice pleaded.

I want that too, I said.

I met someone, she said. I'm moving up north. I'm leaving Veda with my mother till I get settled.

I felt a numbness in my good hand. I said, Of course I want whatever is best for the girl.

She nodded.

Is he good to you? I asked.

I barely heard her. Her voice loaded up like the riders stepping into the cages of the giant disk. Her logic, her love, her farewell, I locked these all up into my own cage. Then out of the corner of my eye, I saw her hand reaching over and I pulled back. Don't, I said. But hearing my own voice broke me down.

智

WHEN THE UNIVERSAL DOORS OPENED, Ip Sik Chew, the ex soy factory manager, and Dai Hou Chow, the ex noodle maker, charged straight to the deli counter. Big Chow asked for a quarter of roast chicken. Don't give me day old, give me fresh, he said.

Every bird is fresh, Ilin said.

Not true, Big Chow insisted. The chicken you sold me last week was moldy.

How about this one? Ilin yanked the hook out of a bird and held it up. Plump like you and still warm, she smiled.

Big Chow adjusted his glasses and nodded. Ilin placed the bird on the board, threw her cleaver down, splitting open the carcass. Then she whacked off the neck and chopped it into three chunks; slid the blade around the wing joint and angled a chop across it so that the thin bones glistened through like long teeth. Ilin slipped the flat of the blade underneath the meat and wrapped up the package. One dollar fifty, she said.

As Old Chew stepped up, she selected a strip of barbecue pork that was glistening with fat pockets, and said, Two dollars.

The men pocketed their pink cones and walked to the Square. They found an empty bench near the chess tables. Old Chew picked up a sheet of newspaper from the ground and started reading.

Go buy a fresh copy, that one has dog shit! Big Chow yelled.

Old Chew flipped the paper sheet front to back and said, I see no shit.

Can't you smell it?

Look what's written here! Old Chew read out loud, Yi-tung Szeto is in deportation jail.

Big Chow looked over and said, Yeah! That's him, with the big forehead, look like a criminal. I have no sympathy for him. Remember how proud he was?

Yeah, he thought he was a big winter gourd, Old Chew said.

So big and heavy. Big Chow nodded. He thought he'd keep all winter long.

Old Chew agreed, Let's see how his dollars keep after he's deported.

Two small boys ran by with pails and Big Chow shouted after them, Don't run!

Don't shout! You'll scare the children, Old Chew said.

You have to, otherwise they'll get hurt, Big Chow said.

Who paid for Gold Szeto's ticket home? Old Chew wondered.

How humiliating if you have to pay for your own deportation, Big Chow said. Don't eat at Sun Wah Kue, it's full of INS footsoldiers, he added. At twelve noon, they order sweet and sour, and by five o'clock, they drop you off at the airport.

Chew Baby, Yoo hoo! The men looked up and saw a blond coming toward them. She sat down and swung her arm around Old Chew. It's Kathy! Me! Kathy Kiernan, from Mulligan's Pub.

Old Chew blinked. You!

Want a date, she coaxed.

He moved down the bench, which she took as an invitation to sidle up to him. No, he said again. No good.

Honey, she winked. Let's make a date.

Old Chew saw that her cuffs were frayed and her coat hem soiled. Her pocketbook was the same hard cornered one she had hit him with once. He rubbed his head. How you do? he asked. Everything pretty good? When she smiled back, he was relieved, smiling made her pretty again.

I do all right. She snapped her gum. Come on, have a date with me.

I no do. He waved a palm back and forth in front of his face and then he pointed her toward the chess tables. Go over there, get a date over there!

She reached into her bag and took out a piece of paper. Sweetheart, here's my new address.

He put it in his pocket quickly and waved her off. Take care of yourself, don't drink too much!

Master Cleaver stopped by and asked, That girlie want a date?

No girlie! You remember that Kathy?

Weepy Woman?

Her.

She was always nice, always said hello with a smile, Master Cleaver said.

Everything got bad after her husband left her, Old Chew said. Do you remember that night Kathy came into the park?

She cried, long as the Yangtze! Big Chow said.

Fur sleeve all wet, Old Chew nodded.

One can only cry so much, Big Chow sighed. Why you get involved with her?

I just try to help her! She drinks too much! She always came around to my factory because soymilk helps her stomach. Every morning she knocked just after I pour the first batch. Sometimes she lost her pocketbook, so I gave it to her, no charge. One day she ask me to deliver, so I took a quart to her apartment and when she opened the door, Wah! she wearing almost nothing. She invite me in, gave me some ginger ale and then she sat on my lap and asked if I like her. But I didn't want to say no and I don't dare say yes and get into trouble. But she saw me thinking and she shrugged, No problem, my husband, he don't care. Then she poured gin into my ale and took my hands, put one on her melon and the other one down there.

Big Chow's eyes widened, Was it silky?

Old Chew smiled, Very.

Soft? Master Cleaver asked.

Softer than flowers.

Wah! The best kind.

Did you lick it?

Slurp! I slurp with all my force, all up. Old Chew smacked his lips and said, Sweeter than my best tofu, silkier than peony petals.

Surely, Big Chow smiled. You will live to be a hundred.

At least! Old Chew nodded. A happy one-hundred-year-old baby.

No wonder your skin looks so fresh today.

She was very active! Old Chew grinned, looking left and then looking right. I couldn't control myself.

Big Chow followed his friends' eyes and then jumped up and shouted, You lie! You tell toilet news!

Old Chew showed all his teeth. Why not?

You pull a big gun! You want it so much you make it all up! Master Cleaver said.

And you two want it so much, you think it real too, Old Chew laughed.

Live for now, Big Chow sighed. Maybe we can't do that, but we can do other things for happy.

Then the men were quiet. A flock of pigeons flew off in a loud and dusty stroke. Old Chew went back to his paper.

Master Cleaver walked up and asked, Have you heard? Gold Szeto's Replacement Wife lost her baby.

Old news, Big Chow said.

Master Cleaver said, Gold Szeto won't have any grandsons.

That smelly egg doesn't deserve it. He never helped anyone, why should I give him my pity? Old Chew demanded.

Master Cleaver shouted, What are you talking about? Gold Szeto made out better than any of us! Haven't you heard?

Heard what? asked Old Chew.

He got away! INS was dragon-dancing, getting signatures on this document and that affidavit, stamping this and stamping that and in the meantime, Gold Szeto got away!

How? Chew asked.

The Irishman had Gold Szeto dead-headed onto a PAN AM flight.

Dead what?

You travel with the pilot, no security, no questions, no problem.

Must have cost a lot of tea money, Big Chow mused.

Worth it. He has his American gold without an ounce of U.S. grief. Heard-told, he'll be opening a Bank of Canton!

Old Chew flipped over his paper, It doesn't tell any of that in here.

No newspaper would dare report it like that! Master Cleaver shouted.

Heard-told, Old Chew exclaimed, that it was his own son Jack who ruined him by going into the Confession Program.

Makes sense. Jack is a bought son, not blood.

Can't expect loyalty there, Master Cleaver said.

He confessed without telling Gold Szeto? asked Big Chow.

Old Chew nodded, Did it on his own.

So he named Gold Szeto as his fake father, Master Cleaver said.

Of course! When you confess, INS will ask you to name everyone in your fake family.

Old Chew wanted to know, What about the Replacement Wife?

What about her? The government don't have proof it was not a real marriage, Master Cleaver said.

Gold Szeto rented the body, but her mind was her own.

A Tigress! Big Chow chuckled.

Shrewd, Master Cleaver said.

Will she and Jack stay married? Old Chew asked.

Who knows?

Who does? Old Chew nodded.

Maybe they have a love feeling. Master Cleaver sighed.

Love, Old Chew exhaled.

There's a bad habit, Master Cleaver said.

Big Chow said, A bad need.

Better to have a big smoke, Old Chew said.

That's breaking the law now, Master Cleaver said.

Love?

Opium, the big smoke.

The men looked around the park, casting for another diversion.

No telling which is the better intoxicant now, Master Cleaver said.

Love always was, Old Chew said.

One hopes, Big Chow mused.

Love.

瑨

WORK SAVED US ALL.

When Joice found work sexing chickens in Petaluma, she called from a pay phone but there was so much background noise I didn't hear much else. Ilin stayed at the Universal with the two new owners. I gave my savings of six hundred to Herbalist Woo and became a street corner newspaper man. Old Woo's stall had been famous for its herbal-teas, but the new immigrants were too busy to balance their damp and dry heat with tonics, so I decided to sell the news. I carried a variety to cover the range of loyalties: the *Chinese Times*, *World Journal*, *Sing Tao Daily*, *China Daily News* and *Mon Hing Yat Bo*. I also carried the *Chronicle*, the *Examiner*, the *Oakland Tribune*, *East-West News* and the *News Call Bulletin*.

The only thing I kept from Old Woo's were the large belly-shaped tonic jugs. When I turned them onto their sides, they were the perfect containers for candies and preserved fruits. I replaced the tops with cork lids that flipped open and shut so that schoolkids could help themselves.

Once we accepted that Joice wasn't coming back any-time soon, Old Lady Qwan brought Veda to the new stall a few times a week. Life was settling.

When Ilin came to me with a request, I was not sur-prised. She had told me this day would come and I had been waiting.

Will you help me find a person, she asked.

What you ask, I can only do half, I said. I'll help you find your relation, but what you do with the information is your business. I kept my word. It was not hard to open my mouth and inquire. My request circulated to relations at the family association, to kinfolk down the coast and a stranger approached me at the Square while I was having my shoes shined. He had a courteous manner and offered the information as carefully as if it were a written docu-ment. The relation you inquire about is employed at the Hoy Hah Shrimping Co., and lives in a white shack off the last pier of the old sea town just past Watsonville.

When I invited him for a drink at the Buddha, he de-clined so I slipped him some tea-money.

I gave Ilin the information and told her, I know you hope that something he says can release you, but don't be heartbroken if in the end, your heart still beats with sorrow. Don't trust that if he says everything you want, that you will be free. Your challenge is unchanged. Hear what you sailed here to hear. Repeat what you hear, but tell it to yourself in kindness. It is still your hand that must open and close that last door in forgiveness.

When I told Louie I fulfilled my promise, he advised that I do one more thing.

She is a woman with child, she is a daughter in grief and her heartache will be supreme. Be a friend, Louie urged. Take my car, he said, You can drive with your right, right?

Ilin was pleased. I drove out of Chinatown, through

the marina into the Presidio, out the Sutro Baths and onto the Great Highway. The water shimmered, green like glass bottles. On the large rocks, sunning sea-dogs barked like burglars. The curving shoreline reminded Ilin of Hong Kong's coastal drive to Aberdeen. She said the clouds were like unpolished jewels and the horizon seemed a palm's snatch away. For a few hours it was easy to forget where we were going and we felt cocooned in the thievery of the moment.

But soon, we were there. I parked on the wharf and we walked to the last pier and found the white shack. The pungent air, briny from the drying shrimp, made me hungry for the old world foods.

I'll wait here, I said.

Come, please, she said.

This was not comfortable for me, I started to say.

Please.

What could I do? I walked with her down the pier to the white shack. Ilin stepped up to the door without hesitation and knocked. An old woman opened it as if expecting us. When Ilin asked for him by name and not by kinship title, I saw the Old Woman's eyes flash with recognition. She stepped aside and we entered the kitchen. There was a round table with two wooden chairs. Dinner was cooking over the stove. Stewing mushrooms filled the room with a yeasty fragrance. The Old Woman offered tea with both hands. Ilin declined it and this made me uncomfortable so when the Old Woman poured another and came to me, I stood and bowed and thanked her. I took a swallow and felt the heat traveling down hard.

I watched the two kinfolk women. Silence kept them strangers. The Old Woman went to the stove, lifted a lid and stirred. I smelled mushrooms. Then ginger and anise, it was an oxtail tonic. We sat in the fragrance and waited.

Soon, the screen door squawked and I turned to see a white-haired man in the doorway. He carried two bags, which seemed to pull down on him like large stones. The Old Woman took the bags and I smelled the brininess of dried shrimp as she passed. The man reached up and pinched off his cap, hung it on the rack, his hands returning to his side like shut scissors.

He looked a long while at Ilin. You are his daughter, he said.

That's when the Old Woman came to fierce life and said, A mirror from the lake would not have more easily cracked glass. What cuts an image of water but its own reflection?

Disturbed by the description of river and glass, I reached for my tea and knocked Ilin's handbag off the table. Was I surprised when her cleaver fell out, when the handle hit the floor like a lost doorknob? We bumped reaching for it but I kicked it hard enough so that it slammed across the room, into the far wall and the colored stones blinked like traffic lights.

Kwan Yin, protect us! The Old Woman ran to her husband and guided him into a chair. He placed his hands on his knees, holding his head aslant for a long while.

I shouted at Ilin, What are you thinking?

The room started to settle, I breathed in the woodsy mushrooms, the steamy scent of rice.

I want repayment, Ilin said.

The Old Man's eyes lifted. He said, In you, I recognize your father at sixteen.

Ilin continued, My father died in your care. You should have honored your brother's body, you should have sent his corpse home.

Now the Old Woman spoke, she nodded her head forward to punctuate each word. Do you want his heart in exchange for your father's? Know this, he would have given it but life and death are not bargains that a man can make. We can only face our circumstance and hope to provide the best road for the future.

Then the Old Man spoke as if pleading toward the blade in the distance. *Brother*, Believe me! I never wanted this to happen. As the elder, I failed you. *Brother*, Forgive me!

Her eyes flashed like daggers. Then the Old Man turned to me and his face bloomed with such feeling, I looked away, in respect.

He pleaded, The situation was not easy then.

I nodded.

It was as if one nod of understanding gave him his strength back. He turned to Ilin and spoke. There is nothing I can say to make you feel better. I can tell you I ran for help, that I begged with the Mexican officials, that I enlisted our family association in Mexico City but there was no way to send the body back. To try and explain those circumstances then is useless now. There were laws by men that collided with laws of our ancestors. Don't believe I didn't want to obey our ancestors. I failed and I have everlasting regret. This is my true sentence. I encountered a situation and betrayed my brother. There is no repayment. I will not ask for forgiveness.

The Old Man spoke toward the ground as if to break earth and reunite with his blood brother.

MY JUDGMENT DAY has come. I deserve your good daughter's anger; she loves the father she never met. I am the bad brother, taking you away from her. Now, I must listen, that is all my worth. Let her blame me, let her accuse me. All I can do is become an ancestor and be the vessel that takes her grief far away, where it will be transformed and delivered as golden light to you. Your daughter had no body to bury, no grave to feed, no memory that comforts. So her rage and grief roars like an ocean, with infinite reach and endless suffering.

Ask your daughter to let me take her sorrow away. Let me take the anger so that her sorrow can find a road to love. Let me deliver her piety to you when we meet in the Netherworld.

Then he faced Ilin and said, My grief doubled because of my shame. And now I see what I always feared, your pain doubled because of my carelessness. I was a bad brother, I am a bad uncle. Is there recompense?

So, the true question flowed through the room like vapor.

His breath filled the room and he completed his thoughts: The Old Woman cried out to Ilin, Your father is dead. Let the story die!

Stop! the Old Man shouted. A lot of time has passed but not one day in peace. He was my brother, you are my niece, your anger can pierce my heart but our blood remains true.

The Old Woman wailed, We have no son, we have no grandsons, and we are alone in the autumn of our life and will be unremembered in the afterlife. Is this not punishment enough?

Ilin was weeping now. I went to her but she turned her back to me so harshly, I stepped back. I filled myself with thoughts of my own mother and I waited for love and solace to fill me. Then I realized it wasn't Ilin I should speak to but the Old Man and I turned to him, not knowing what I was going to say. I opened my mouth and the words arrived.

Listen, I said. We have all traveled a long way. Let's forget the sorrows made from traversing the worlds. You could not protect your brother in the new land and your suffering, like hers, has been immense. Be unified in your loss; it's all the same.

Then the smell of the mushrooms filled the room, as potent as the words we dare not repeat. We let the fragrance of earth soothe us, calm us, intoxicate us.

The Old Man waved for Ilin to come closer. When she didn't, he spoke from his seat. Make the good life yours. Live well for your father, live better than your Uncle.

Uncle. The word of blood.

I was not prepared for what came next. Ilin's declaration fell out of her mouth the way her cleaver fell out of her handbag—intending harm—but in truth, a catalyst to confession. She said, I have a new happiness inside me. I will have a child.

Rage was dissipated by sorrow. All confessions led to new life.

The Old Man said, It would please me if you brought your child to meet his Great Uncle.

Ilin moved to him and wrapped her hands around his.

I saw the effort in her eyes as she called up every kindness she'd ever felt, every goodness she'd ever been given. She looked full into the Old Man's face and said, Be well, Uncle. Then she turned and left. I followed her down the stairs out toward the long pier. And under the descending clouds, I knew she would never be back.

WHO COULD SAY why? Not long after that visit, Ilin lost the baby. Louie gave me the news, not Ilin, and it was Pegeen who told Louie. This was just the way trouble came about, no one talking direct to the other.

That Sunday, I took Ilin out to PlayLand at the Beach. We walked through the Funhouse, which was packed with family and tourists. Fathers pitched dimes onto towers of slippery plates at the game tables and young kids pulled on pinball machines. In the center of the courtyard, Laughing Sally held court. She was a nine-foot robot with red hair, dark freckles and blinking green eyes. Her heavy brocade dress was ripped and the dangling patches of sequins rustled against the wooden stand as she rocked back and forth. Sally pitched back and forth, her wooden jaw snapped.

Ilin shuddered, Is she crying or just laughing?

She's just crazy, I said. Then I led her toward the set of illusion mirrors. In front of the first, Ilin's body stretched out like a rubber band and she glanced back at me, her face open again. I stepped in front of the next mirror and my body spilled out of the frame. My face widened into a winter gourd. I smiled and my teeth enlarged. She burst out laughing and I abandoned myself to it as well. Then I got on the Conveyer Walkway and she followed close behind. We bumped and bumped, pedaling one step forward and getting pushed back three, always in the same spot.

She called out, How come we're not moving?

The road of life, I answered.

We got off and as we walked pass the Shaking House, a bunch of boys tumbled out like drunkards and Ilin said, We don't need to go in there. So I took her downstairs to show her the photographs made of human hair and mounted birds, both of which she found upsetting, so we left.

Outside, I led her up the hill toward the ruins of the old Sutro baths. The burnt cinder odor from the big fire was still strong and acrid. As we stepped down, the blackened foundation crumbled. The tide was low as we headed down through the old foundation. Pools of water were thick with algae growth. I led her along the outer rim, stepping over the rolling pools, walking along the narrow ledges toward the edge of the cliff. On the Big Rock, a seal arched and lifted its head, it began to sway but I couldn't hear its bark because below, the waves broke and crashed like a house demolishing.

I stood there and felt myself bearing the tremendous sea force. My trousers billowed out like sails, like a promise. I watched the waves crashing white against rock and threw my gaze out into the horizon.

She said my name.

I looked at her. Her hair blew forward and her hands raised up in supplication.

I told you when we first met, I would ask for your help.

Again? I asked.

Help me bring my mother over, she said.

How?

I want to leave the marriage intact so my mother's paperwork clears easily.

The sea air bit. I told her I understood her determination.

She paused and then said, I can help you with Veda until Joice returns. A girl needs a woman nearby.

I watched the waves rolling in infinite whiteness, the salt bite gave me resolve. As you need yours, I said.

Yes, she said.

What did I have to lose? What was there to fear? I was only afraid I had no place, no soul to deposit my good will. We've already walked this far together, I said.

Her thank you was soft as mist.

I kept my eye on the setting sun and just before it disappeared, I saw the flash of green, a leaf of time, a receipt of infinity.

BUT IT WAS not to be.

Her mother passed before the paperwork cleared. Ilin came to me, pulled out a telegram. My mother died alone, she said. I failed to keep my promise.

That wasn't so easy, I said.

All that caused her grief was now laid out like a banquet. She told how her superstitious clansmen forced her dying mother out beyond the village walls, that she died, sheltered only by a makeshift bamboo shed.

It was a pitiful story and I didn't know what to say. What word would comfort the aggrieved?

中習

IN NEARLY FOUR YEARS, Joice had been down to San Francisco no more than three times. I still hoped and so I waited and Veda waited but it was Old Lady Qwan who said to stop waiting. Boredom will make idiots of us all. When Veda was four and ready to start school, I registered her at Jean Parker School on Broadway. Old Lady Qwan walked her there in the morning and at two thirty, I picked her up. She was helpful and liked stacking the newspapers and then the quarters into piles. Every Saturday, we walked down to Yip Tang Trading Co. by the Stockton tunnel. She always stayed on my right and I understood my ghost hand frightened her. So I called her my Left hand Minister. And then like a minister, she walked up and down the aisles, advising me on the difference between bubble and chew gum, which baseball cards were most popular, what type of taffy pull-candy, thin or thick licorice, sweet tarts or juju dots, orange slices or spearmint and what color cotton candy.

Soon she insisted on walking to the news stall herself

and because she was popular, classmates followed her like a school of fish. When they pressed their faces against the large jars, the late sun hit the thick glass and their smiles reflected back like happy carp. Veda tucked her books away and served her schoolmates herself, scooping out the candy, weighed and calculated the cost and then made the change. She was only eight but her math skills were impressive and I could tell she had a natural talent for business and I left her in charge while I did errands.

Once, while I was across the street getting noodles, I watched as she confronted a boy. She jabbed him in the chest and though she barely came up to his chest, she wouldn't stop until he handed over a pack of cards. I was proud. My girl cut through adversity like a shark, teeth first.

Ilin was embarking on a new life as well. Brother One and Two had sold the Universal to the Double Eight Hong Kong Investment Group. Ilin quit before they could fire her. She tried a few take out delicatessens on Stockton Street and the FourFiveSix Noodle House on Dupont, but no one was interested in a lady butcher, especially one with her temperament. Pegeen had just quit the fortune cookie factory to work with Louie at the Buddha, so she introduced Ilin to Manager Chee and Ilin started making cookies.

Every evening that rainy April, Veda and I went to Joss Lane to pick up Ilin who was always behind in her production so we waited in the alley. Veda liked how the store smelled like toasted almonds. Ilin sat in front of a black machine that Veda called a giant spider. The oven was the belly and there were eight arms with round cast iron griddles at the ends. When Ilin pressed down on the foot pedal, dough was squirted onto a griddle and as these rotated into the oven, one would stop in front of her seat. She lifted the edge of the hot cookie and slipped a fortune in its center and then quickly folded it once and then pressed the half circle over a metal bar. Done, the toothy shaped cookie hardened and she threw it into the box. There was another box, the imperfects, that was always the fuller one, which she had to buy. So Veda and I were recruited to eat the misshapen and fortuneless cookies till the roofs of our mouths were sore.

Ilin's fingertips were red and peeling and every day she swore to quit, but I reminded her of the earlier, seemingly insurmountable discomforts: how ice cream was too cold, the Broadway hill too steep, the butcher cleaver too heavy. Time made gold of everything, I said.

WHEN VEDA WAS eleven, Joice returned to San Francisco with a new boyfriend; they moved into an apartment on the upper Grant and even though it was only minutes away from Chinatown, she could have been in another world. Veda was fascinated by her mother and was always waiting for her call or visit. When Joice came around, I found her distracted. She always had a strange smell around her, sweet but medicinal, like a stale tiger balm. She wasn't as quick as I remembered. Sometimes when I asked a question, it seemed a long time before she found her answer. I found myself saying often, You seem lost in thought but inside, I realized maybe she had found what she was looking for, Joice was lost in love.

Veda liked Joice's clothes, her soft blouses with elastic sleeves and necklines, bugle-bottom pants or loose skirts that either reached the ground or rose high and tight around her thighs. Joice took her to the park at Washington Square and Veda came back with a crown of daisies, which she wore till the yellow petals dried out. She asked for a toe ring and an ankle bracelet and refused to wear shoes all summer.

But it was Ilin who sewed the soft flowing clothes for Veda and Ilin who took her to Yone's Beads on Vallejo and taught her how to make chokers, long earrings and beaded necklaces. Ilin crocheted ponchos for Veda and braided her hair with five plaits. It was Ilin who taught her how to pay respects to her elders, how to ask me indirectly for the answers she needed, how to listen out of time, how to ask the forgotten questions.

In all, it was Ilin who comforted us all.

巼

OLD LADY QWAN'S ASCENT into becoming an
Ancestor was sudden. Wong Moo told how they
were both sitting by the swings on the lower level of the
Square, that the sun was beaming, the metal chain links of
the swings flickered like firecrackers. Old Lady Qwan was
talking about where to get the best mooncakes, how to
crimp solstice dumplings when she called out to a boy trying to stand up on the swing.

Don't fly! Old Lady Qwan shouted and then she
grasped her heart, slipped down to the ground and left our
world.

THERE WAS no answer at Joice's apartment, so Veda
stayed with Ilin that first night. She begged me to take her
to the cable car barn where she believed her Grandmother
was waiting. At first I said No but then she cried so hard, I
acquiesced. We walked up Washington and stood outside
the barn, listening to the wide echoes of the churning

motors, to the engines roaring in huge voluminous breaths, to the gears cranking and crashing like an earthquake.

Veda cried and cried and I let her. There on Taylor and Jackson, surrounded by echo and fury, I gave her my secret and my promise: The dead loved deeper than the living.

THE QWAN FAMILY WAS dispersed. I had heard that the only brother was a street bum. The Tenderloin or the Mission, no one was sure, so for two nights, I walked both districts before I found him at midnight on Polk and Geary, scrounging the garbage cans of a Thai restaurant. I offered to take him for a meal but he refused. I told him about his mother and said arrangements had to be made and he said, Let Joice. When Ilin found the twin sisters in the East Bay, they had the same response. Ilin was horrified and went to find and help Joice. I told her not to meddle. I knew Joice would be outraged but not surprised, Even in death, she had to attend to everything.

I closed the stall, picked up Veda's dinner and took it to Wayne Alley. As I came around the bend, I saw my daughter's face at the window and was reminded of the little girl I saw on my way out of China, the girl with the wind-chime voice, the child who followed me out of my home village.

Veda too, was always waiting, in doorways, by tables, against the window ledge. Her eyes aimed at me like a bayonet. When I walked into the apartment, she started crying for her Grandmother. Veda too, had the same chime voice.

I told her, Your Grandmother is dead. Tomorrow we say goodbye to her.

Why is Grandmother dead? she wanted to know.

I looked at her and said, Grandmother was old, it was her time.

How old?

So old, she had no more time, I said.

Veda was quiet long enough for me to think she would leave me alone.

Then she sang out, Dad? Is your arm dead?

Don't be so annoying, I said. Don't ask so many questions. I went to get her dinner. She followed, still talking, still asking. She pulled up a chair, her breath as hot as a racehorse. Are you old, Dad? she asked.

I looked at her eyes pooling, her lips pursing, all her features lifting up in supplication.

Dad? Her voice suddenly hoarse as if she had aged, her breath urgent as if aching, When? When are you going to die, Dad?

I set a cold hard look on her and she slid off the chair and went into the bedroom. When her dinner was ready, I called for her but she didn't come so I went into the bedroom and found her bent over the headboard, a crayon in her hand.

What are you doing? My voice was thief-harsh.

But my daughter smiled brightly and moved aside to show me what she had done. I looked at the headboard and saw that she used red crayon to fill the name her mother carved onto the headboard. I yanked her off the bed and I shook her with all the might of my one hand. I couldn't stop. Not even when I saw myself in her terrified eyes.

Do you want my blood? Do you want my last breath?

I paid everyone back. I lost everything. Where is my fair share?

Just what do you want? Tell me! Tell me!

I gripped her shoulders, digging my fingers in till I felt her collarbone like a bar of bamboo. I shook her. How hard? Her head rocked and lolled. How long? She bunched up, light as a dried bundle of bamboo leaves. I dragged her out of the bedroom and threw her onto the couch, cursing and cursing, not releasing my grip even when her crying became all swallows and gasps.

Every regret, every swallowed shame spread through me and then I felt the power of my lost hand rise up as if my fury manifested another fist.

Like the wild mouth of a river gorge, my daughter roared for her Grandmother.

I gripped her shoulder and I shook her.

Do you want to live?

The echo of all my words beat back at me. Her teeth chattered as if cold. Her loose hair flew back and forth like sheets of seaweed. I took her shoulders and pushed her. Her hair flew straight up. I yanked her back and her hair dipped around her wet cheeks and though horrified with the distortion in her face, I kept yanking and then pushing her, trying to line her face back with her hair, trying to balance us back.

Do you? Do you want to live? Do you want to have another day?

Her tiny fists thrashed at my throat like a hurt sparrow. And then her eyes bore into mine, her pupils grew.

Stop! she shouted. Stop or I'll call the police!

It was not her words, but the steel in her tone that made me stop.

When I saw my daughter's tear-streaked face, I averted my eyes. How old was she? Just twelve, but already, in possession of all her mother's fearlessness. Then I realized it was true, our children do pay us back, they do return us to the original place where we faced our last and maybe our first true selves.

I too had once been like her, desperate for my mother's return, of body, of love. Every child wanted to return love to the ancestor as every lover wanted to be loved eternal.

She was right to threaten me, maybe she should have reported me. Soon enough, she would not be the daughter in waiting. She might wait and want but not getting, she would leave and I would be the Father in wait. Already, I felt a shame greater than any sorrow I had ever known. I feared that I had spent all my goodness.

When Ilin and Joice walked in, I had already released my grip, but the pain and confusion was still static in the room. Only then did I hear the sobbing of my child and then I could only watch as she ran to both mothers; I could only watch as they took her away without a word.

At the Buddha, Louie sided with the women. When he asked, Why are you so hard on your girl? I did not oppose his opinion and so my disgrace doubled.

I KNEW it was a feeble apology, but it was the best I could do. I took Veda and MiMi, Louie's daughter, to Sears Roebuck and let them pick out a favorite toy in hopes that a happy memory could consume the sad one.

MiMi chose skates right away but Veda walked every aisle three times, touching dolls, board games and trying out jump ropes before she selected the skates too. Ilin joined us at the lower level of the Square and we watched the girls circling the sandbox on their new skates. In the sandpaper stillness, Ilin mentioned that she and Manager Chee were spending more time together and I understood, love was slipping away again.

The girls skated past, their metal wheels rang and their gasping breath was like summer rain. I watched them, happy they were having fun

Veda skated up fast and threw herself into my lap, her laden legs kicking upward. MiMi squealed as she whisked past and Veda jumped up, posed with a pointed wheel and shot off after her.

Be careful, I shouted.

Ilin called the girls for lunch.

Veda and MiMi were racing around the playground now, backs bent, arms reaching, mouth screaming.

Let them have fun, I said.

They're breathless, Ilin said.

I called to them but they circled us several more times but wouldn't stop so Ilin and I stood in their path and caught them. They threw themselves on the bench. Ilin laid out newspapers to sit on and moistened towels for their hands. Then she pulled out two sticky rice packets, peeled back the bamboo leaves. The girls held them like bananas. Their legs kicked under the green benches, their eyes wide and their long breaths, happy and content.

I watched Ilin peeling a peach. She scored the skin and then skinned back the thin furry quarters, handing each girl a perfect sliver.

The sun was strong and there was a steady breeze. The girls were laughing. I trusted life to continue in this triangular fashion.

I hoped Veda would do well living with Ilin and that Ilin would heal with a child in her realm.

I let them love. I understood there would be many dangerous crossings and I trusted Ilin to guide us both.

ilin cheung

I T WAS CLEAR after Old Lady Qwan was buried, that Joice wasn't capable, interested or likely to be a good mother so I invited Veda to live with me. She was almost fourteen, the time when a girl should be close to a woman. I was pleased for Veda's immediate acceptance and also for Jack's approval, but I still wanted to talk to Joice. So I left work early and walked over to Old Spanish Alley where I knew she would be cleaning out her mother's apartment. The drizzle was steady so I watched the apartment from under the awning of the Grandview Theatre. The door swung open. Joice walked through. She was wearing a see-through raincoat, shiny boots, fishnet stockings and a tall hairdo under a bright headband. Her A-line dress had a bold pattern of pink circles and orange squares; the bright colors worried me, they were not appropriate for a daughter in mourning.

I flipped open my umbrella and stepped into the street. A car sped by and I felt a quick slice of heat along my legs but kept moving until I reached Joice. Her fake eyelashes gave her a surprised look. A thin white stripe over the heavy black liner gave her an exaggerated expression.

Hello? she said.

Her lips were pink and icy which made her look more bereaved.

I told her I was sorry for her loss.

When Joice lowered her eyes, I searched her face for a likeness to Veda but couldn't see it. I said, I want to talk to you about your daughter. She looked up, expectant, which I attributed as inner feeling for her child.

It's better she live with a woman than with Jack. What's your feeling? I asked.

Why didn't he come himself? Joice asked.

When I saw how she twisted her lip, as if she were locking her words in, I saw the Mother that was and the Daughter that would be. Defiance was the resemblance.

Then Joice's lip twisted and she said, Jack can feel but to speak is another matter. You don't need my permission.

I want it, I said, surprising myself with the force of my statement. I had meant for it to come out as request for a blessing.

It's fine, Joice said.

This isn't an easy time, I offered. Then it started hailing, the drops hitting white and wide on the pavement. I lifted my umbrella and Joice stepped into the offered shelter.

As I recalled my own heavy loneliness those first months after my mother died, I remembered what she taught me: *When helping a man in difficulty, do it as you would save a fish from dry land, do it as you would a bird from a fine net. Do it while there is life.*

So I told Joice that I'd waited a long time for this opportunity to participate, to be a friend, to be like a family.

Joice smiled as if it was something she'd heard before.

We walked out of Old Spanish Alley and up Jackson. I

kept her company while she ordered flower wreaths at the florist, bought butterscotch candy at Woolworth's and then at Ming Fat's as she selected white envelopes that would hold both gifts: sweetness in farewell and a silver coin in gratitude. After getting rolls of new dimes at the bank, we went to the Qwan Family Association. As Joice was settling the purchase of the burial plot, she broke down. She was sobbing so hard, I led her outside, took her in my arms and told her, Let go.

She let the rain wet her face, her tears mingling with the heavens.

Rain was our steady language. The language of tears fixed the unknown between us.

I was surprised that Joice was working the shift before her Mother's wake but I didn't comment as I walked with her to the fleabag theater on the corner of Stockton and Broadway.

Her smile was sincere as she thanked me. I watched her walk through the double doors; I turned to go and then stopped in front of a poster. Two women embraced in the foreground, a man watched them from a distance; his distraught, distanced expression made me wonder why it took so long for Joice and me to meet face to face. And I wondered, If we had met under different circumstances, would we have chosen each other as friends?

囧

IN THE MIDST of our new triangular peace, news came that Louie was ill, gravely so. When I'd commented on his coloring, Louie revealed nothing. It was Pegeen who told me it was cancer. Then Joice gave me the herbs and the recipe to ease his time. You have to adjust it, she said. Chocolate might be too bitter for Louie.

I went to Ilin's to use her oven. As I was boiling the beans and heating the herbs in butter, there was a knock and then I heard my name and knew Edso wouldn't stop so I went and cracked the door and shooed at him. Go to the Square! But he stuck his foot in the doorway and yelled out, Jack Moon Szeto! Are you in there counting your dollars?

The butter was about to burn, I could smell it and hurried back into the kitchen. Edso followed me, sniffing like a doe. What are you stir-frying? What smells so fragrant?

I'm making cake for Louie.

He peered into the pan and sniffed, Is that Dai Lum? Why butter? Chinese never use that.

Butter brings out the *boo* qualities. Like quail with ginseng.

Boo what?

Stomach cancer, I told him.

Edso shook his head. That's very bad! Can he eat?

This will help, I said.

Edso snatched my sleeve. Don't catch yourself on fire!

I drained the softened lotus beans, broke three eggs, poured in the crushed walnuts and sugar and then handed the bowl to Edso.

You're lucky I stopped by, Edso said. He mashed everything up with a big spoon and then took a taste and deemed the bean paste as good as Hop Kee's.

I rolled the paste into balls and flattened them slightly.

No crust? Edso asked.

More potent this way, I said.

We Chinese used it first, Edso said. It's written in our Yellow Emperor's Classic of Internal Medicine.

Louie is a good friend, I said. When I was heart-broken, he made me squirrel wine. Now I make cake to break his pain. I slipped the pan into the oven, set the timer for twenty minutes. We sat at the table and had two shots of whiskey. I noticed Edso looking over his newspaper and casting a worried eye on me; after the second time, I asked, What's the trouble?

How old is Veda? he asked.

Almost sixteen, I think.

He hemmed and then said, It's none of my business, but as your friend, I am obliged to report things I see concerning family.

What? I asked again.

I saw your girl at the pool hall, she was not a good girl.

I know, I said. I was there.

Then you saw her with that Crumb-boy?

Chee! If you saw, everyone saw.

Edso nodded, embarrassed too. Very, he said.

We stared at the oven, listened to the timer ticking.

Did you do anything? Did you scold her? Edso wanted to know.

What could I do? I didn't want to shame her in front of so many people. It's my fault, I was not a good father.

You weren't that bad, Edso said. Plenty fathers worse than you. Look at Mankok, three wild girls, a boy in that Bad Boy gang! And what about Louie's daughter? Inside the pool hall, I saw her fooling around with one guy and outside, I see her with Fourth Fong's youngest son!

The one that was in jail? I asked.

He must have gotten out, Edso said.

Maybe I failed to give Veda enough direction, I said. I gave her my trust but maybe that wasn't enough.

Maybe, Edso murmured. But even if you did give more, you could still have the same outcome. Character, like talent, is heaven-mandated.

I said, Maybe I shouldn't have confessed, maybe things would have turned out better.

Why did you *hon pak*? he asked.

For Joice, for love, I said.

Love is the only risk worth more than gold, Edo said.

The timer rang and I pulled the tray out. Edso peered over my shoulder and said, Ha! Moon cakes without a crust! I try!

Take it, I said.

He wrapped one up in his blue handkerchief. Hot, he said.

Go home, I said. Stay home, I cautioned him. Don't go talky-talk all over the Square.

*   *   *

EDSO DID GO to the Square and he did talk and what he got was the Crumb-boy's story. Every family had one, an unwanted son, the useless brother. His name was Noland and he had just arrived from the Sacramento Delta. His was the typical bad-seed story, boy gets into trouble, boy is sent to live with faraway blood-thin relations. But trouble followed Noland to San Francisco, where he got mixed up with the gangs.

Veda never officially introduced him and I never questioned her about the incident at the Lambert's Pool Hall despite the fact that I had to endure customers coming to the new stall to tell me about the same incident. If I had been old world, I would have confronted the Boy's guardian but this was a modern situation and I wanted to deal directly with the boy. Every afternoon, he and his band of hoodlums passed by the news stall on their way to Moy's Sweets so I had a chance to study him. He was muscular from his martial arts training but his eyes were soft and I knew his heart had a long way to go before it would be built up like his body.

Already, I knew Veda overpowered Noland. He had not yet developed the resources to fend off her desire or her dominance.

One afternoon, I saw the boy coming up the hill and just before he entered Moy's Sweets, I called him over. Though he stopped, his band of hoodlums lined up around him and he waited a bit before sauntering over.

Do you speak Chinese? I asked in Chinese.

He nodded, almost obediently.

Then I have a few things to talk to you about.

He shrugged.

What are you studying at school?

He looked down at the ground.

Listen to me. If you want to be friends with my daughter, I have two conditions.

He jammed one fist and then another into his pants, as if to say, I might listen, I might not.

I'm trying to help you. I waited till he looked up. If you care about her, if you want to make her happy, I won't be the obstruction. The first, You must study. The second is this. You must break with those Crumb-boys.

He looked at me, not defiant, but bewildered.

Do you understand? I repeated.

He shifted his weight before nodding and then walked away without farewell.

Words on the tongue are best resting there. I didn't call him back. Pause is often the gift that invites a better reincarnation. Our conversation never found its way back to me and this pleased me. He was a boy who already understood honor. I believed I saw the coming-man.

NEAR NOON that Saturday, I headed to the bank to get change. It was still overcast and the flat light magnified everything. There was a rush and rest rhythm on Stockton Street. People moved like magnetized puppets, tourists lumbered like large caged animals. Trucks and cars and buses were packed in a line of exhaust fumes all the way to the tunnel. At Jackson, I stood at the crowded corner, waiting for the light to change. Orange Land was packed, two customers deep. Big Al was gripping four oranges in each hand and the ladies were giggling. A truck pulled up and Al filled two bags and lifted them up to the window.

That's when I saw Noland approaching the Stockton corner. He was alone and he was smiling, I remembered that. Suddenly there was shouting and I turned and searched through the crowds. When I finally saw the butchers, they were charging out from the crowd. I didn't see their hand truck till they got to the intersection and I didn't see the stack of pigs until they reached Noland. Their long hair hid their faces and their tight head movements were unnerving. Then people were yelling and running and things were overturned, cars were honking, the bus hissed and braked and the world cracked.

I could barely breathe. I could barely believe. I had been wrong, they were not butchers; they were only boys. They threw down their trolleys, tore off their white coats and reached elbow deep into the gutted pigs, drawing out long melon knives.

A woman screamed and Big Al jerked around and his sacks ripped open and oranges were banging down the sides of the truck, bouncing into the gutter.

As if one body, the crowd bore back in fear and then surged forward, in morbid fascination—howling—every mouth open in horror.

The Egg Cake Lady's cries filled the street corner and broke our trance. *The long-haired one, that one with a mole on his left brow, that one was treacherous, the way he pulled his elbow back, the way he socked the butcher knife in and then pulled it out, as if to cut out the boy's heart! Look how the wet blade shimmers like cash.*

I ran to Noland and lifted his head. His mouth was working in a slow chew, like a caught fish trying to eat air. The crowd surged over me but not one man lent his hand, not one woman prayed to our Goddess of Mercy.

Where was our mercy?

I pulled him onto the curb. Hold on! I yelled and then sprinted the half block up to Chinese Hospital. Two emergency workers followed me back, carrying the folded stretcher down the hill like a surrender flag.

ONLY THE *News Call Bulletin* printed a photo. The grainy black and white image showed Noland slumped on the sidewalk and me reaching under his shoulder, trying to lift him. In the background, a sea of mouths and eyes poured over us like a jury of fish. From the upper left edge, a figure is breaking into the picture's frame just as the shutter snapped. It is Veda and her face is wild.

The *Chinese Times* misprinted his name. It used the character *Dream* instead of the character *Hope*.

I was surprised how this upset me. When young life is stolen, one wrong word deepened sorrow like ten. The *Chinese Times* should have gotten his name right.

His family did not come down from the Delta.

Sorrow jumped somersaults and then came our sour years. My daughter blamed me; I bore each accusation. I let her.

I could do no right. My tone was wrong, as was the way I looked at her. My advice was old. I knew nothing new.

I was grateful Veda trusted Ilin, as did I.

My daughter was learning the new language of womanhood and her frustration was bearable. I trusted that her youthful ranting would wear away her fears.

As Louie said, Let time.

智

I DREADED THAT coming moment when MiMi would deliver the news that her father was back in Chinese Hospital. And like morning, it arrived. I shut down the news stall, got the cakes and went to the hospital. It was the dinner hour and all the corridors were filled with cots, the nursing stations were empty and I walked two floors before I found my friend. Asleep, he looked more sunken and more pale and my breath caught in my chest. When his eyes opened, I slipped the silver box into his palm and whispered, Big Smoke. I clasped my hand over his. Brother, however it eases your time.

Then I peeled back the foil package to show him the cake. Good for your stomach, I said. When Louie bit into the cake, the dark bits of bean that fell onto his chest were rich as earth.

Lotus? he asked.

Special made, like squirrel wine, I said.

We let the words fill the room.

Then Louie's eyes held me and I asked, What is it?

His voice was so bare of breath, I leaned forward to catch his words.

I don't have much time, he said.

I felt our past filling the room and I looked into his eyes and saw his present drifting. My throat seized up and I waited till the words found me and then I waited for my breath to steady. I swallowed and asked, What can your Brother do for you?

Help yours, he said.

I didn't understand; I waited.

Louie's voice kept breaking but his sentences continued to build. Be mad at your old friend but don't be mad at your girl. You're too hard on her.

I didn't know what to say.

You know what I'm asking you to fix.

His hand twitched and I wrapped it tighter around the silver box. His eyes opened, thanking me. Then his voice was weak but stern. Your girl wants to hold a common story with you. Don't make her sacrifice love to chase you. Fix that. Otherwise life doesn't lead life.

垚

WE BURIED Louie in Colma, in a section of the cemetery that had previously barred the Chinese dead. Lim P. Fung, the famed geomancer, chose a site that rode along the uppermost ridge of the dragons' back. Shaded by a majestic fifty-foot Chinese elm, Louie's final resting place faced eastward.

Pegeen would manage the bar until MiMi turned twenty-one. We were pleased when MiMi took over the Buddha, and even more pleased when she kept it unchanged.

When Manager Chee and Ilin bought a house by Golden Gate Park, Ilin and I dissolved our paperwork. I moved into the apartment on Wayne Alley. Water rushed over rock, my current of life swelled and I carried on.

Veda was at City College and working part time at the airport. The few times she asked for advice about school, I couldn't advise her. When American Airlines offered her a job, it was a transfer to Boston and she came and asked what I thought she should do. What could I tell her? She was nineteen, she had a whole life I knew nothing about, lived in a world I couldn't imagine. I told her, It's up to you. You have to figure that out. I said, Your father trusts you.

Her mouth twisted downward, she had that look like she was going to cry.

My answer was wrong but my answer was spoken and it was too late. What could I do? I sensed this had not been her true question so any answer I gave would have been deadly wrong. Something didn't match, how she looked, what was coming out of her mouth. I knew something serious had happened. I waited. If she wanted to tell it, she would. She already couldn't ask direct, I couldn't afford to push her. I had to let my daughter lead.

I understood, sometimes a child just wanted to be close to the parent.

As her father, I wanted to say something, give her something to hold onto for later. So when she started gathering her things, I took a deep breath and called her by her baby name and said, Whatever it is, nothing is worth unhappiness.

She put her head on her lap. Then her tears came like a flowering. I waited and when her eyes lifted, I saw my child again and I called her by her baby name.

Tell your father what is making you unhappy.

She shook her head. I knew she was hurt and this hurt was not something that could be talked through.

Are you ill?

The way her head shook made me cringe as I remembered how I'd shaken her in a rage.

Your Father has suffered in the hope that it would have been enough so that you would not have to. But that would not be fair to you. Whatever you suffer, your father gives you the courage you need to break it.

We let those words fill the space between us.

That winter, she left for Boston and her life in the harsher climates, away from the family fold, changed her. Eventually, she resettled in New York City and like any traveler, new places made new lives. Those years, we were not close but I trusted that discord would soon enough be dissipated by distance, it was natural law.

BECAUSE OF Veda's flying benefits, I got accustomed to her just showing up and so the night she called to announce her arrival, I was surprised.

We're going to the INS, she said. You're getting naturalized.

What for? I told her things were fine the way they were.

Things could be better, she said curtly. See you tomorrow.

I held onto the weighty receiver for a while, listening to the wide horn of sound. Though I didn't like any contact with the government, I didn't like disagreements with my daughter more. I didn't think about it anymore till Ilin showed up at my news stall and asked if Veda had called, I knew they were comrades on the matter. Ilin droned on about the benefits of her own naturalization and boasted, This isn't changing allegiance, this is adding to it!

Loyalty to state was not loyalty to blood, and the latter was not to be had in an oath, I said.

She stood up straighter as if to insist on her new loyalty as an American and said, Cooperate! Don't be a troublemaker.

You're the one always making trouble, I said.

She pinched her waist, she threw her eyes at me; I was forewarned. But I wanted to ask, What happened to your shy glance, your tender bride voice, your soft hands that could not grip a cleaver? When did you learn to roar like the Great Mean Tigress? But I withheld commentary because the one thing I learned was to let a woman ask and answer to her heart's content. All women liked the sound of their own wailing.

She barked into my ear, Do you hear me?

I stepped back. Mao Tse Tung heard you!

Mao's ears are green! she shouted back. His corpse *faat mo*, he's moldy.

I laughed. Then it's a good time to go back to China, the old salted egg is dead.

Fix your papers first, she said. What if you go back and don't like it or more likely, they don't like you? Then she smiled, But if you do want to stay, you can have your Social Security deposited into the Bank of Canton!

You think of everything, I muttered.

She didn't hear me because she was bellowing, Tomorrow, lunch at Hang Ah Teahouse and then dinner at my place. I'm soaking a shark fin, Veda needs it, her face is more wrinkly than a shar-pei dog. Sea cucumber for you, no cholesterol, good for your high blood pressure.

Ilin's face was scrunched up so tight, I thought hers was the wrinkly-dog face. When she patted my head, her calloused fingers made me pull away. I asked, Didn't you say you were going?

I am! I leave! I'm going to the Bank of America, do you need some quarters?

Got plenty, I said. Then I watched her moving up the hill, marveling at her strong gait and I thought, The ancients were right, the future was grand because the view from the aged terrace provided the ideal amusement.

Friday afternoons were always busy, so I moved quickly to get the stall ready. I filled the candy and fruit jars to the brim and put out extra papers. I stacked up quarters and dimes. Then, waiting for the crowds, I read about the coming summer heat, the falling price of gold and about the son who chopped his father to death because the old man refused to buy him a playboy-car. There was a huge racket and I looked up and watched the driver trying to reattach the cables of the Number 30 Stockton. That's when I saw my daughter across the street. I set my patience just as I had weighted down my newspapers. The light changed. Veda cut through the peopled horizon like a blade. She moved like a shark, with a long stride, a determined glance and a destination. I felt proud. My daughter had found her way to walk in the world.

She greeted me with coffee and a book.

What's this? I asked.

Study questions for Monday.

I ignored her helium-high voice, her forced-happy expression and flipped through the book. There's over a hundred! I shouted.

They won't ask every question, only a few of the important ones, she said.

I sipped my coffee. What's to prepare? I go as I am, I said. Her eyes were as focused as a general's, her mouth set as if chewing back words too large. I observed that her attack was too ambitious, she had no plan for a successful retreat.

Edso Lim, usually the first to run off at the sound of discord, came drifting up from Dupont, exactly when I needed his irreverent conversation.

You! I greeted him.

He assessed the situation and pulled a milk crate up to Veda. You come to see your Godfather?

Of course! Veda smiled.

You make a hundred thousand yet?

More! she teased.

So you invite Godfather to a wedding banquet yet?

Nope.

Not yet? He reached for a *Times* and said, Let Godfather read you some love-ads.

No thank you, she laughed.

Edso shouted, Wey, Jack Moon Szeto! Why doesn't your girl want a husband? It's your fault, you must be a bad father.

Who's a bad father? Jimmie Chan handed me a quarter.

He is! Edso pointed at me.

I gave him a look to mean, Don't bring up the past. I didn't want Veda thinking about Noland, which she might still blame me for.

Jimmie! Where you been? I asked.

Cuba! Jimmie said.

You pull a big gun! I said, Nobody can go to Cuba, it's against the law.

I go, Jimmie beamed.

You talk from the bottom of the ocean! Edso said.

I do not! Jimmie said, I be in Russia too.

Edso asked, What's fun to do there?

Moscow has a big Chinatown. I go there.

Edso asked, There's a Chinatown there?

Jimmie threw his arms out in a wide arc as if calling for an audience to gather. All over the world, he shouted. Every country has a Chinatown and I go to them all!

Edso challenged, How you get there?

Jimmie lifted up on his heels, I took a taxi!

How you tell the driver? I asked.

I draw a picture, Jimmie said.

Smart! Veda said, Drawing works.

What kind of picture? I asked.

Jimmie opened his palm. He said, I draw a street, then

I put Chinese people on it, then some storefronts with a big sign, then I write some characters, up and down, make like a real Chinatown. I put Chinese people on the street.

What kind of clothes they wear? Veda asked.

Jimmie puffed up. Northern clothes, big sleeves, padded jackets, everything long to the floor, everything tied with belts and then I draw a big fur hat.

Edso laughed, That's how Northerners dress, all tied up. The taxi driver, he know?

No problem! Jimmie nodded. He know and he take me there.

But how you pay him? I asked.

Jimmie showed a ten bill and said, I gave him this.

He give you change? I asked.

He give, Jimmie nodded.

Then what you do with the Russian money? Edso asked.

Jimmie's eyes brightened, I use it on the way back.

Edso gave another thumb up. Wey, Jimmie Chan, you really can-do!

Of course! I be a seagull, I go everywhere. Jimmie looked at his watch. OK! Time to pick up my girls. I see you people tomorrow.

I had a line of kids wanting nickel bags of candy and adults asking for current journals so I said, I work now. But every so often, I glanced over and saw my daughter on her milk crate and I yearned for our old days together.

At closing, the three of us closed the stall in no time. Edso and I broke down the shelves and stacked the boards over the crates. Veda dismantled the postcard and magazine racks. I was impressed with how quickly she tallied up the returns and that she remembered how to slash diagonally along the front page, how to tie up the dailies and which corner to stack them for pickup. When she lingered over the gung fu novels, I told her to take one but she only quickly boxed them all into a milk crate and slid that under the shelf. When everything was tucked and piled into the narrow closet, I pulled the accordion door and padlocked it. The three of us stood before the wooden closet that was my business.

Dinner, Veda asked.

Edso swayed back and forth, waiting.

You come too, Godfather, Veda said.

No! I shooed at him, You go!

Veda invited him back, but Edso had the sense to decline. I have a card game, he waved and moved on.

Win big! I called after him.

Lee Gardens or King Wah? Veda asked.

Two people at a banquet table were ordering up pity! I pointed across the way and said, Why not Sam Wo?

Her face lit up as we headed up the narrow staircase. I saw how her hand lingered on the worn banister. We went up to the top floor and she went straight to her favorite table and stuck her head out the window.

Be careful! I shouted and saw my little girl again, at the window watching for me to turn that bend in the alley. I ordered simple dishes, steamed tofu, hollow spinach and her favorite rice noodles.

The dumbwaiter bell rang.

Where's Old Jue, she asked.

Moved to Arizona. I didn't have the heart to tell her that her favorite waiter was found dead in his room.

Hot there, she said and watched the waiter removing our dishes from the black box as if she were seeing it for the first time. We ate in a home-silence that was satisfying.

*   *   *

DUPONT WAS EMPTY and we walked, her arm linked through mine, with only the soft sound of footsteps and a pleasing sensation. When we entered Wayne Alley, our silence was like an old blanket. We passed the condemned building on the corner and she pointed at the old cars in the lot and said, The rust will eat them before the city will tow them. The gas lamps flickered and cast her silhouette against the building. Inside, I warred with telling her something. When a red cat flattened itself and slipped under the fence on the other side, my daughter turned back to smile, and I walked up and said, Your friend Zhenren Wu came to see me.

Really? her brow raised. What did he want?

To tell that he cares for you, I reported.

Really? she repeated. He wants a family but I don't. Her voice was almost defiant.

I would not betray the hope of the man who traveled a distance to declare his love for my daughter. I didn't tell her that he asked for the details of my ancestral home and that he hoped taking Veda there might be a blossoming. He came to me as a Man and I wanted to honor his belief. Though I had taken that trip and it had not worked out for me, my daughter deserved her own travels.

What do you think, she asked.

My duty was still to protect her heart so I said, He seems sincere.

Her eyes bloomed. Chance opened like a palm and I seized the opportunity. Happiness is the goal, I said. Everything is worth that.

Her smile was the first surprise and then her kiss, the sweet second. The Ancients were right. In youth, a man found the companionship of a woman enlivening. In his middle years, a wife nurtured him and in his autumn, fulfillment came from the tender companionship of his child.

I drew in deeply, so my peace arrived. To have my daughter return and tend to me was contentment beyond compare.

I stroked her cheek. See how it goes, he seems a good man. Then I watched my daughter move with liquid grace down the alley and felt a coming peace.

Longevity was the unmapped road ahead.

智

WAITING FOR the women, I had several cups of osmanthus tea at Hang Ah Teahouse before Ilin showed up at eleven thirty. We have to talk, she whispered. Do you know what your daughter is doing?

I poured her tea and asked, Doing about what?

Ilin's face pinched, proof that some thought was pickling her. Better you ask her, she said.

Why don't you just tell me? I said.

How come you don't know? she asked.

What should I know? I asked.

Your girl might break the law! Then she set her lips like there was no parting them.

Which law? I wanted to know.

Does it matter? She snapped back, Law is law.

Is she a prostitute? I asked.

Ilin coughed up her tea. Don't say such bad things! I didn't say she was a Bad Woman. That would be worse than breaking the law and if that were true, would I be talking to you about it in a teahouse? Then she lowered her voice. It's that boyfriend.

Wu Zhenren? I asked.

She drew back in surprise and then laughed, His name is True Man? Is he a communist?

I kept it simple and only told her that the young man had come to pay his respects. I didn't mention that he wanted the name of my ancestral village or that he wanted to understand why Veda was against having a child; our meeting was business between men. There was an unfinished story here and I knew that Ilin sometimes rushed to the finish without all the facts. He cares about her, I repeated.

Ilin bit her lip. Do you trust your daughter is smart enough? Do you trust she won't get swindled, fooled, robbed through the heart? She pulled at my arm and when my empty sleeve fell out, she acted annoyed and said, You should let me stitch this up for you.

Same as what we all want, Luck and Love. I tucked my sleeve back into my pocket.

Ilin snorted. There are givens by nature of the environment he came out of. Even if his love was true, his true hunger might be more powerful.

Her comment made me pause. Ilin herself had made use of my position for her own better gain, but I held my tongue because she'd earned my loyalty; because she was good beyond measure to Veda. I smiled and said, In the same vein, I could forgive you.

Have I asked? she teased back.

You should, I insisted.

Wait till I do then! Then she tucked her softness away. Did he have a devious look? Did he ask for money?

He had manners enough, I said.

Manners are not money! You better do your duty and say something fatherly.

What's fatherly? I asked.

She mumbled, You have no clue, her top lip settled down over her lower like a dumpling lid crimped to seal the morsel held within.

A waiter refilled our teapot, splashing water.

Let's order, Ilin said. It doesn't look good to sit with nothing on the table.

She called for our preferred dishes: blood pudding, phoenix feet, tripe; sticky rice, dishes better eaten before Veda's arrival. Eating blanketed our rising unease. When I glanced at Ilin sucking on her chicken claw, I thought about how we had earned each other's comfort and company. Ours was better than a real marriage.

There she is! Ilin called out. I caught Veda's eyes casting like searchlights over the teahouse floor. My daughter glided toward us, slipping around food carts and singing waitresses. I pulled out a chair, Ilin poured tea and we called out for Veda's favorites: leek dumplings, turnip square, taro root. We did not talk; there were only the satisfied sucks and swallows that proved our familiarity.

Veda put down her chopsticks, took a swallow of tea and said too loudly, Naturalization is a convenience, you can go back to China and still have the option to return.

If I go back, I won't return, I announced.

Veda looked lost.

Ilin yelled, Don't be so stubborn.

I knew naturalization was not the whole story, I saw that something else had an unreasonable grip on my daughter. I saw it in her unsettled gaze, how her lip twisted downward; I knew her mind was warring with her heart. Her expression reminded me of the character "to think." I had taught it to her. I told her it was a unique ideogram, one that was made up of three separate characters: tree, eye and a heart. *To truly think*, the heart guides the eye. The heart sees, the eye thinks, the forest is alive. The forest in Veda's life was a battlefield between her eye and her heart but there was no time to teach her otherwise because right then she started the Great Examination.

Veda asked, How many stripes on the flag?

13, I answered.

Veda continued. Name the ship that brought the pilgrims.

Fifth month flower, I answered.

Mayflower, she corrected. Use English, she commanded.

Mayflower, I repeated.

Then she laughed. Here's one. What immigration and naturalization service form is used to apply to become a naturalized citizen?

Chee! Now you bullshit your father.

Look! She flipped through the book. See? It's written right here: Form N400.

I shut the book and said, Since I answered all your questions, it's only fair you answer mine. Ilin said you and that Wu Zhenren want to go to China and make trouble.

Wey! Don't damn me, Ilin cried out.

My daughter fidgeted like when she was a child sneaking candy to bed. He's already married for his green card, if that's what you're worried about.

Ilin gasped. He's married?

Was, Veda quickly corrected.

Why does he want you to go to China with him?

He's doing a favor for a friend. She isn't legal so she can't leave the country and can't afford a babysitter so she wants to send her babies back to China.

Babies back to China, I said. Today the world has changed.

For the grandparents to care for. Veda held up her hands, Two babies.

Ilin frowned.

I didn't see what was against the law about the matter, but I kept my mouth shut. Ilin and Veda had an eye-war and I stepped out of the conversation. Veda was staring at her plate like she was ready to bite it. What woman-secrets they were communicating, I did not want to know.

Let's not have an incident in a teahouse, I said and flipped my chopstick over and used the top-end to select a bright green stalk and laid it in Ilin's bowl. The emerald stalk languished over the white mound of rice. I chose a leafy stalk for Veda. Then we were speechless and I could almost hear the minutes marching by, an army of wasted ammunition.

I wanted to say something simple and clear and soothing, words Veda could tuck in a branch of a tree, in her breath, in a swallow.

Guard your heart, I told my daughter. Nothing is worth unhappiness.

She pursed her lips like how she fought back tears as a little girl.

Ilin smiled like a dim-sum cart-girl. Noodles with young chives? In season and very yummy!

The teahouse racket poured in and we hid under the din of lunch-noise like an extra blanket.

We just sat—three heavy melons in a patch— ignoring each other until a waiter came and flipped the lid of our teapot. Behind me, I heard men arguing about the benefits of returning to China.

Don't be reckless, one man said.

Another shouted back, Stand on all sides and think carefully! The communists are treacherous.

Worse than the INS footsoldiers of the '60s!

Old Chew saw me and shouted, Jack Moon Szeto! Would you retire in China?

Of course! I shouted back. The Motherland is our final paradise!

Deafness was the unknown drug for immortality. I half listened to the men, bantering about returning to the homeland and to Ilin stacking and restacking the bamboo trays, calculating the tab. One side of the table was paranoid, the other side, defiant. I looked around the packed dining hall and observed plenty of operas and realized all our troubles were more bearable in this noise-wok. Against the background of a thousand other troubles, how unusual was ours? I saw my daughter as I first saw her mother at the Great Star Theatre, a ticket girl as addicted to romance as Lin Dai-Yu in *The Dream of the Red Chamber*. I saw Ilin as a fearless warrior from *The Water Margin*, pointing a quivering sword at a phantom enemy. Cymbals and gongs announced my entrance as the one-armed swordsman. Gravely wronged, but powerless in retribution.

Ilin and Veda started fighting over the bill. The check tore, the green bills fluttered and we were in a new, unnamed opera.

A congee cart rolled by, one loose wheel rattling wild on the linoleum floor.

Veda's eyes lit up. Congee? Do they have liver?

I ordered it for my daughter. The server set the bowl down and the porridge was steaming with iron chi.

IV

return

回報

TO YI-TUNG SZETO

Dear Husband:

    I write to tell you that your letter and monies have been safely received. Your Old Mother is very happy indeed. As to the adoption of the son to continue the family line, we have already gone ahead with our plans. You must understand however why this matter took some time. This is a matter of utmost importance and rules had to be followed. We had to wait some time for the right person. Now we have chosen a descendant from the ancestral line of Chin, he was the long son, the last child. The boy is now five years old. He has a flawless and upright countenance, healthy in mind, a child right after our own heart. Your third Uncle acted as the middleman. Upon your approval, we are planning to name him, Yuo Seen. We have consulted the fortuneteller and decided that the ninth day of the ninth month is an auspicious one to receive the boy into our family. The contracted price is $410; including the commission for the middleman, the expenses for the ancestral ceremonies; everything amounts in total to about $500 American.

We should have notified you earlier but did not only for fear that the secret might have leaked out before the transaction was successfully executed. Therefore, the delay.

We have chosen the ninth day to adopt the boy into our family. Our ancestors can finally close their eyes in peace. The family will take a photograph together at the autumn moon festival and will send it to you as soon as possible.

We used the remaining monies to buy mooncakes for the family. We will light a lantern for the festival. Everyone here wishes you a happy moon festival.

That is all.

Your True Wife

true wife's lament of infertility

THE BOY WAS delivered to me, wild with grief. I locked all the doors because he kept running away. His reserve of tears was so great, I sealed the windows and let his sorrow flood the house; I let him lament. I let him have his cleansing cry because I understood his grief. Like the candle that consumes its own heat, his tears consumed his fury. He cried full and fierce as I had wept over my own barrenness. I knew that when our crying mingled, our tears, like ashes, would absorb our sorrow. My prayers to the Goddess of Mercy would be answered; I would become his true mother.

Then I will hold him, then I will nurture him, then I will love him more deeply than if he had come from my own womb. I equaled him in heartache. My sorrow of infertility was as fierce as his loss. I was barren, he was forsaken. But because our Kwan Yin flowered merciful eyes and bestowed me with joy, I tried to soothe his wailing. I told him, Don't think about her, she was a bad mother, she did not want you anymore.

He howled like a wild dog. My mother is good. My mother is good!

Your mother did not want you. Call me Mother, I am your mother now.

He charged at me. His small fists had compacted strength and I was bruised. He hollered, You are not my mother! You are a duck-webbed ghost.

I grabbed and twisted his wrists but he bit my cheek. I cried out, Why so vicious, why so mean? Up close, his face was streaked with salt lines. That woman did not want you, I murmured. I want you. I am your mother now. I coaxed him, Call me Mother.

He broke away with the force of wind, wailing. My mother is good! My mother is good!

The house was a storm. He screamed like the God of Thunder. I was afraid he would drown with his endless weeping. But I saw the good. He was proud. He was loyal and I rejoiced in this truth; he had been loved.

Let him have his fury. Let him rage at me. Let him believe that I was the robber-thief of his heart; this only proved that he knew what he lost. Let him mourn, let him grieve, then maybe he will not have a bitter eye.

I called upon my ancestors for forbearance: *Love rejuvenates, love regenerates.* Love does. Love does.

I imagined his crying as a mountain song and went about my work. I cut our famous river noodles, silken from the clear flow of mountain rain. I hung the fresh strands over the bamboo poles to dry, gathered up the dried strands and tied those with red string. All the while, I was quietly attentive to his every movement and felt him watching me as intently.

For three days, he refused my meals. I stilled my heart to match his in beat.

When he yelled, I yelled back.

When he was silent, I kept quiet and soon our quiet roared like one single ear.

Fatigue overcame him. His thief-eyes followed my every movement and soon he did not see me as the enemy but his unborn feelings terrified him.

The third evening, when the sun was setting over the mountains and a band of late light slipped in through the window, I started making the soup. I stirred in the oxtail, the celery, the onion and ginger and last, dipped in the ribbons of noodles. I had given him a pheasant feather and he waved it back and forth like a ribbon, seduced by its iridescence. He turned away when I brought him the bowl, but I saw him lick once and swallow in anticipation. I stirred and the anise and ginger bouquet burst like a flame into the darkening room. I brought up a wiggling noodle to entice him. Eat! A belly of food is more satisfying than a belly of fire. He turned his face away so I put the bowl on the table and said, I leave it here for you.

Outside, I went to fetch the evening water and kindling. Hunger overtook him and soon, I glimpsed him tasting the soup. I felt great relief but I dared not allow my gaze to linger. There would be time enough to readjust his chopsticks, to caution him that a child who held his too high would become a traveler. My fear became the lesser hunger. There would be time to pierce his lobe like livestock, so that he would be rooted to earth and not stolen by son-thieving demons.

When his chopsticks crossed in midair like pincers, when his mouth puckered over the bowl's curved rim, when he slurped in hearty gulps, I breathed a sigh of release. His dignity was young. His hunger was old. But I knew his surrender would give us our eternity.

碧

THIS IS a story I'm afraid to tell and afraid to keep. I gave it to Louie and asked him to take it to the Netherworld. This is a story I will never tell my daughter. This story should only be told to a lover.

A son about to embark on the road made a last visit to his parents to offer thanks. The marrying daughter served tea in gratitude and departed; the arriving daughter-in-law served tea in new allegiance. Bride and Groom vowed one hundred years of love and promised the Ancestors an heir. This was rule, this was the rite.

Before I sailed for the Flowery Kingdom, I went to pay respects to the woman who gave me life. I traveled to Sand River Village and found the house with the almond tree and I waited under its shade. A brood of kids played barefoot in the dirt courtyard. The younger girl saw me first and called out to the older boys; they stopped kicking at a paper ball and ran toward me, waving their dirt-caked palms. I reached into my pocket and threw a fistful of hard candy at them. The colored pieces skipped like stones and the boys pounced on them. Then all three pairs of eyes were afire and three pairs of legs were flying toward me. They cried out, Money! Money! I dropped a half dollar into each dirty palm and they ran off, their laughter as hoarse as thieves.

Only the girl stayed behind, the coin aglow in her palm. Stranger, stranger, she called, her voice soft as early rain, Who are you?

I'm a traveler passing through, I said.

Her eyes sparkled like river stones, her bare toes marked lines in the dirt as if drawing a map. She dipped her head and looked at me with inverted eyes. Traveling where? Her laughter was like a wind chime in Autumn.

To a faraway land, I said.

Then I felt a pair of eyes fixed on me like a sword of sunlight. I stared at the house till the house blurred and my stance swayed. I waited a long time but there was no sound, no movement.

Que. I thought of that word that described the unusual coincidence when dream joined desire to create a mirage of hope. This was such a moment. *Que.* Whether for pain or in shame, the woman who gave me life refused to come and face me, even as a shadow.

What choice did I have? I shut the four chambers of my heart, pushed love and regret through like a tortoise and set out on the only road before me. I let my shoulders rock, I let my elbows swing and I walked out of the old world.

Where? Where is the Traveler going? The girl with the wind-chime voice sang out after me, and ever after, this wind-girl became the harbinger of all my loving. She was the guiding breeze through Joice's defiance, Ilin's boldness and now Veda's determination. A woman gave me life, this would always be the first gift. And each new woman I surrendered to, love would be the second wonder.

Perhaps what the ancients say is true. The man who is given a child opposite of his nature is luckiest. His patience is tried, his character is tested and his spirit is rejuvenated.

Like the girl with the wind chime voice, my daughter edged at my patience, waiting and wanting something that was not mine to give. Watching me from the milk crate, waiting for me at the doorway, hanging onto my every word, always wanting to slip in that question about my past. It was wrong for Joice to tell Veda my story; this was a story between lovers, this was not a story between father and daughter. My daughter did not need to swallow my sorrow.

My daughter held this story in her belly till it became Anger. And she held this like a deity. Fidelity or fury, her loyalties were extreme. I wanted to teach her how to release herself into the middle temper.

What I wanted her to know was this: Telling can be a detour. Telling does not necessarily invite completion. No story matters till it is finished and the only stories that need telling are the ones whose endings do not fulfill us. I wanted to tell her, enlightenment was a flame, one only needed a pinch of light to dream by.

Now, my daughter returned, a woman on fire, a Fire-Woman who could make a lie the truth. She was the daughter who wanted to take care of her father. She asked me: Will you get naturalized?

Will I?

A new plant becomes naturalized to a new land.

Maybe my daughter hopes naturalization will give me the safety to set root.

Maybe my naturalization can give her a sanctuary in trusting that her father will not be deported.

As when my mother took me across the river and handed me over to a new home, I stood before a new road. I want to free my daughter of any obligation to my history. Whatever I endured is not hers to ponder; how I survived is not hers to wonder; she will come upon enough heartbreak in her own life.

Protection, I said. Trust yourself.

My story is native to our history but it need not be our root. A naturalized plant is new life. So I hand over my story. Let her tell. Let her not. Let her find her way through the story so that it frees her.

v

release

veda qwan

I ALWAYS REMEMBER IT as my first story. My mother told it to me on my birthday. She took me to Fong-Fong's for a celebration, ordered me a float and then told me his story: *Your father was sold to a woman who couldn't have babies. The village was so small, its name was a number.*

I didn't like how her voice was foamy like the root beer so I pushed at the vanilla scoop until the bubbles and cream overflowed the tall glass.

Then she told me her real news: that she was moving up north with her boyfriend and that I would live with my Grandmother. When she promised to come for me once she got settled, I said I didn't believe her and I didn't finish the float.

Grandmother claimed I cried and refused her noodles three days straight.

Hunger is no good, she said. You need something in your stomach. You need something to sit on the hunger, she said.

Hunger was the reason. Hunger was the proof. It answered why my father was sold.

So it was hunger too that got my mother to tell the story that freed her from the family fold. She told and she got to go.

When my mother came to see me in New York, I took her for soup dumplings in Chinatown and then for coffee at Vincenzio's. I let her finish her decaf and then I asked why she told me his story and why she was back in my life now.

So that you would have the resources to love him, she said.

Resources? That's an odd word, I said. You should have trusted me, I loved him on my own. I sat with him, afternoons and evenings and weekends and I listened over and over again to how he was always the best. He was the quickest dishwasher, the fastest wonton wrapper, the best roaster. He made perfect rice, clear broth. All the boogaloo women chased him, shop girls and bank tellers and waitresses fought to serve him, waitresses slipped him extra dumplings and at the telephone exchange ladies knew his number by heart.

I knew the truth was what he didn't tell. His stories were always about how he was the favored and pursued and preferred. I finally figured, No one told him he was loved, so he had to keep telling it to himself. I'd tried once, I said. When he was at Chinese Hospital for an appendectomy, children weren't allowed to visit so I'd asked him to call me and all day, I'd practiced singing Happy Birthday in Chinese. But when he called he was curt and dismissive. I sang anyway, holding the phone so close, my breath spooked me. I barely finished when his quick goodbye came and then the line was dead. So I learned, intent is important only to myself.

When I asked her what she wanted from me now, she confessed her guilt about him losing his citizenship and now wanted to repay him by getting him naturalized.

How's that going to help him? Does he want it?

She shrugged, He's been talking about going back to China, they all do. This will give him options, she explained tentatively. He could travel back and forth if he wanted. Naturalization would give him freedom of choice.

My mother's insistence was surprising. Guilt really got a grip on her. She forged his signature and put in his application. She also suggested we not tell him till the time came. No point in giving him the chance to work up his fear, she said.

Why not you? I asked

Are you kidding? He doesn't trust me!

Inside I thought, Neither do I. It was a good enough meeting and then she was gone. I almost forgot about it until she called me about nine months later with an appointment date. Timing was good, I'd quit American and was finishing up a temp assignment as the Community Outreach Coordinator at Chinatown Newcomer Services, a fancy name for English-speaking receptionist. Then I had a trip to China with my boyfriend and it all timed out, I could be in San Francisco the weekend before his interview.

My office was on the sixth floor above the Canal and Baxter triangle. We had huge windows and a wide view of the busiest intersection in Chinatown. For lunch, I liked to pick up hand cut noodles from Marco Polo and bring it back upstairs to eat by the big windows; it was like TV, watching the street traffic and the tourists haggling with the street vendors. There was a good looking guy with hawk-like features that I always looked for. He didn't have a stand of fake designer bags or a floor-store of movies and videos, he just stood there, opening his long coat to a steady line of customers. He had a jumpiness and I kept expecting him to bolt and then one day, he did. He shot across Canal and headed down Baxter. Two cops in dark dense blue were starting a sweep. It was easy to keep the Chinese guy in sight because his unbuttoned blue shirt flew behind him like a bright sheet of river. Around the corner, he slowed and even though I couldn't see his face, his stride told me he was smiling.

That Friday, after a steady stream about late utilities bills, rental disputes, missing Social Security checks, that same Chinese guy walked in and somehow I wasn't surprised. His name was Zhenren Wu and the cops ticketed him for selling without a license. I advised him to pay the ticket and then to apply for a permit. When he gave the noncommittal, I'll see how it goes, I was irritated. It was my father's same ill advised logic of the world. Something else got to me, his mannerisms felt familiar in an unsettling way and I realized it was about Noland. Zhen had the same cockiness, that pigheaded need to slip through, a fearlessness about living outside society and a disregard for the law.

Pay, it's worth it, I advised again.

He handed me a card.

I laughed when I saw his name. True Man?

Is that so funny? he asked.

The card said he did Tui Na massage and I almost asked how many jobs he had but remembered how Louie rented out his garage in triple shifts so I knew the answer. Some things never changed. Chinatown was still the first Eternal City.

I told him I'd always wanted to try Tui Na but was suspicious of the Chinatown places with women hawkers at the door. Are you any good? I asked.

Come judge for yourself, he offered.

I did go and it was the weirdest massage I ever had,

but he was very, very good. His teacher was an old blind woman and she'd taught him, her hand over his. When he kneaded my back, pinching down each vertebra and then nearly yanking my arm out of its socket. When I felt my blood rush, it was all worth it. When his knuckles pressed into points in my skull, I gasped and then I couldn't resist sneaking a look and was surprised at the sexual intensity of his expression and I bit my tongue.

You're really tight, he said. Then he started telling me about his only perfect patient. He said, His body was open, fully oxygenated and I could get in at every point. Later I heard that after he left, he was hit and killed by a bus.

You're scaring me, I said.

The man's body knew, it was already prepared for death, Zhen explained.

Lai-hoy, I mumbled.

Dangerous. We laughed at the word I chose but it would become dangerously true. His massages were *lai-hoy* and I would get addicted, which was to say I got into Zhen. He had an order to his universe, a line of continuity about people and relationships and just plain living. I never had that. I had expected his to be the life-in-progress, but his was actually the more settled life. He had a culture that rooted him. Of course, his China-buggy ways irked me. He belched, his first take of tea was loud and he was bossy. I didn't like that he smoked, but I liked how he looked doing it, his legs double crossed like a helix, very third world. But it was his hands that I fell in love with, how hand over hand he made everything connect.

We got together quick. Zhen started picking me up from work and we would go to his place on Mercer (a loft-sit for a friend of a friend, he was full of unexplained luxuries that way) and he always had some snack or rice plate or a special herbal soup. I felt safe with him in that way I had felt safe with my Grandmother. Evenings became weekends and then I was at his place more than mine.

I wasn't surprised he'd had a green card marriage and I wouldn't have been surprised if he told me he was a father too. He wasn't, but the ex-wife, a runaway, was practically a child. When he started telling how he found her scrounging trash bins on Catherine Street, living under the Manhattan Bridge, I stopped him and said, I know you're a good person and so I don't need the details. Besides, I said, all this tells me is that since you're already a permanent resident, we don't have to get married.

He gave me an amused look, the same odd smile when he showed me his real work, a project about calligraphy. Zhen did huge character calligraphy based on his study of foreigners who had lived in China. The first in the series was twelve-by-twelve-foot square and based on Matteo Ricci, the Jesuit who introduced Christianity to China in the late Ming.

When I complained that I couldn't read any of it, he said it was meant to be about confusion.

I'm interested in how Ricci broke through the Chinese sense of greatness, how he studied our language and created a memory palace to teach it to others, he said.

I looked at Zhen's created script, hard lines boxed in characters that looked like rows and rows of brick. Rigid, I said.

Like China now, he said.

Like Chinese people all over, I mumbled.

Giuseppe Castiglione, mid Qing, he said. I like this one better, I said. Though barely a tracing, the characters were all sweeps and curves, the radical components on the left like manes, with small brushstrokes below like galloping hooves, just like Castiglione's horse portraits that hung nearby.

I can't read it, I said.

That's my point, Zhen said. Language wasn't about reading, it was about seeing. He told me that all his work was the repetition of two lines of text taken from the Grand Historian Sima Qian's letter to his friend Ren An.

A man has only one death.

That a brave man may not always die for honor, while even a coward may fulfill his duty.

I shrugged. Why make up a script when one existed already? I asked.

The old one doesn't work anymore, he said.

Those two lines have such an old time sentiment, I said.

Chinese loyalty is eternal, he said.

Then what about Norman Bethune? Edgar Snow? I asked.

I'm avoiding the communist period altogether, he said.

That's smart, I said.

ONE NIGHT he made me a special dinner, chicken with black mushrooms, a dish my Grandmother always made for my birthday. He even ate it like her, a slice of mushroom atop a sliver of chicken, to enhance the taste. There was also an herbal lamb brew to boost my system for the winter. He laughed when I scooped up globs of oil with my spoon and picked out all the goji berries with my chopsticks.

What's up? I asked, knowing special foods had a special purpose. That's when he told me he'd agreed to escort a friend's baby back to China and asked if I would go along.

When I asked why the mother didn't go herself, he started in about how she wasn't legal, couldn't leave. I stopped him because I could have told it myself. Woman had a baby from some misguided belief of legal security, woman sends baby back to China to be raised by grand-parents. Baby grows up very mad at the world. They pay by time or by baby? I wanted to know.

A thousand five a child, two babies, from separate families, he said. Traveling with a woman would make it easier. The last trip, the little boy cried from New York to San Francisco, his face pinched like he'd been ripped from the womb. *Zhen Que!* he said.

Truly Que. I was truly surprised. Zhen used the ex-pression I had only heard my father use. Zhen even said it with the same curling astonishment as if calling up marvel and worship for the unknown. I never knew its exact meaning, but from the tone, I had assumed it expressed the absurd and wondrous synchronicity of how life met life.

As if ripped from the womb.

I brooded on that phrase. I heard a voluminous sound like how the sea echoed from a conch shell. *My father's mother sold him.* My voice stunned me, what I said was warbly as if it had ridden in from the far sea and then as if my body was catching up, I heard myself mumble, I guess that would be my grandmother.

That was common in the old society, he said.

I DECIDED TO go for the money. But when I got to Hong Kong, I shut down. As I looked across the harbor and Zhen pointed out China, I was paralyzed with dread. This was before I had any inkling of what Zhen had planned, it was just a gut feeling, I just did not want to be anywhere near China.

Zhen held up the babies and insisted. The train was packed and noisy and smelly, the countryside was depress-ing and the boy's howling gave me a headache and I was glad when we dropped him off. But smiley Xiao Mei was hard to hand over, she gripped me and twisted her lip and then came her awful cry.

After that, I was ready to go home. But only then did Zhen tell me we were headed for my father's ancestral village and that he'd arranged for me to meet my father's blood-mother. I was shocked. I didn't bother asking how he found her because I knew how. Talk. Everything was by talk. Talk was the highway through history. Talk conquered time. Talk was blood through eternity. Zhen talked till he found the oldest member of the village and then he just asked.

He held the car door open. What could I do? I was in his territory. I got in and slammed it so hard, the tinny Citroen shook. I didn't say a word the whole four hours we drove along the back roads. Out my window, I watched construction gangs working on the new Four Districts Expressway. It was a scene from the last century, half-naked men hunched along the dirt road, hand-hammering every inch of the new expressway. I was reminded of the crazy Chinese bum who rode the Number 30 Stockton bus from the Terminal to the Wharf. I would see him in the morning, and then again after school, still in the same seat. Every day, his chant was the same. On Broadway, he'd cluck his tongue at the topless posters of the burlesque queens. At Orange Land, he'd shake his head and ask, *Why do these people work so hard? What kind of karma do they have?*

Downtrodden Chinese in the States was a sight I was used to, but seeing the same in China was upsetting. On that long stretch of back road in Canton, I kept asking the same question: Does it ever get better?

Our driver swerved through traffic like a whip and I kept getting thrown against the door. My shoulders tensed up and I got scared, remembering how my collar bone snapped riding next to a fat lady on the Switchback at the State Fair.

Out my window, the road was a bicycle circus. Bikes were crammed with tall bamboo frames. Geese and ducks and chickens were tied so tight onto the lattice frame, they looked like a woven feather tapestry. Two bicyclists transported twelve-foot ladders, stopping traffic on the five-lane road. A father cycled his whole family, toddler on the handlebar, wife riding sidesaddle behind him. Zhen and the driver puffed one Double Dragon cigarette after another and I chewed through three packs of ginseng gum.

When the car pulled up to the old stone gate, I got out and walked right through the stone pillars and looked down into the trickling stream. A water buffalo was tied to a tree by its nose ring. Its tail swinging back and forth like a wand calmed me and I stood by the beast as if it were my bodyguard.

When Zhen came and put his hands on my shoulder, I shook them off.

It's important, he urged. You should.

Should. I told him, I hate that word.

One is not alone in this world, he continued.

I looked out at the necklace of mountains and felt lassoed in by iron and rock. The sternness in his voice only made me feel more trapped. I crossed my arms and then uncrossed them. It's hot, I said.

She's family, he urged.

I twisted my lip, wishing I hadn't lost my paper fan.

Once, he negotiated. It's only right.

How do you even know she wants to see me? I demanded. But I realized the real question was, Did I want to see her?

Zhen answered it. You're blood, it's natural law.

Under the direct midday sun, my head felt constricted, as if I were wearing a metal helmet. I turned a full circle looking for shade. All around, people chattered in dialect which annoyed me even more. I started toward the river, Zhen followed. People put down their work tools, children stopped kicking their paper shuttle-balls, old men rose from their wicker chairs and leaned on their canes to listen to us.

Zhen's voice deepened. Be the kind one. It's how you are human that will bear witness.

I turned and jabbed at his chest, Don't *should* me. So we entered our own battlefield, this was about us. Zhen and I had no middle ground. He wanted a family, I didn't. He hoped that if I met family, I would reconsider. But in the motherland, where selling babies was not a moral crime and could be excused for its ultimate ancestral obligation, my resolve not to have a child only deepened.

I walked away from him, past a row of houses, their tiled roofs the same slate gray as the surrounding mountains, and I thought about how in this ancient hamlet, whole lives were still trying to bloom. The road turned to dirt and I wound through the rice fields, then sat down on a rock by the stream's edge and dipped my hand into the water, enjoying its refreshing coolness. A moment of ease. But then I heard footsteps behind me.

It's up to you, I won't *bik* you, Zhen said.

To force. Bik was a spiked lock clamping around my neck. No! I shouted. You just tricked me! I turned away.

A woman walked toward us from the fields, her fluid grace mesmerized me. The tip of her long hoe peeked over her shoulder like a sword and its metal pike glinted. She swayed as her weight sunk into the earth, the soft churn and suck of soil like a small dog running alongside after her.

Sister, she greeted me.

Too shy to reciprocate in kinship kind, I only nodded back. I observed Zhen and her in conversation. Her cautious smile paraded from politeness to curiosity and his voice warmed and loosened. So I understood how his sense of family rose from the land and I heard how his language and tone was its natural tribute.

The woman put down her tools and dipped each foot into the clear stream and then unhooked the straw sandals from her waistband and slid her feet into them. She offered to take us to the Ancient One and we followed her through the center of the village and then single file down a shady lane. The wet stones were slippery and a fish odor rose from the gutter that ran alongside the narrow pathway. Barefoot children ran after us into a dark lane, their chanting eyes as menacing as beggars. She stopped at a white stone house with the roman numerals 55. I followed her through the low framed door into a large square room. In the center was a high brick bed and in that deep center was a small figure. Zhen introduced me as the granddaughter from the Flowery Kingdom. I approached the bed, feeling shy but also feeling an odd shame for being a stranger.

The Ancient One's wide eyes were buried in wrinkles, a thin edge of blue rimmed her irises.

Zhen repeated the proper address twice but the kinship term felt false to me. Hello, I said.

Aye. The Ancient One's voice cracked like a new layer of ice.

Then a tall girl entered the room carrying a large teapot by its flat bamboo handles. Her mother followed with a big platter of food and summoned the Ancestors. *A whole chicken to call forth the extract of a good life! A whole fish to invite prosperity. Oranges bright as carp! These, our gifts to the dead.*

More people entered, setting their offerings on the table under the portraits of Ancestors. Bundled babies were deposited on the bed and toddlers climbed up and cozied close to the Ancient One. Everyone sang out greetings and then sat down on chairs arranged along the eastern wall.

An elderly man burned incense, reciting the names of the dead. The girl and her mother handed out bowls of rice and everyone stood in line to partake of the blessed offering. I watched a fly atop the chicken start cleaning itself, its glow-blue wings like glass. When the young girl brought me a bowl piled high with the three foods, I tapped my chopsticks to the chicken and then touched them to my lips; savoring its essence. Tasting saltiness was safer than taking a bite.

When I asked the mother how we were related, the whole room roared in laughter and I was reminded that in China, humiliation was something I had to get accustomed to. The mother shook her head and her bobbed hair glistened like a raven taking off. Officially, she explained, waving her hand toward the wall filled with portraits, I'm your Grandfather's youngest brother's wife's sister's second daughter's cousin. I tried to follow but felt my eyes crossing and would have laughed out loud if she hadn't directed me solemnly, You can call me Ah-Seem.

But the honorific would not leave my mouth, so I just smiled.

Having set up a line of blood evidence, Ah-Seem shouted an order to her daughter, Pay respects to your cousin from the Flowery Kingdom.

The girl's detached expression told me she was already an immigrant in mind. She ignored the command and leaned over the bed, her long arms snapping like shears as she lifted the Ancient One to a sitting position. I was in awe of how graceful she was.

Not necessary, I deferred.

Not necessary? the mother thundered at me. What are you talking about? This is proper custom!

Forgive her, Zhen interrupted. She doesn't know our custom, she's like an orphan.

I glared at him.

The mother skewered her daughter with a scowl and then threw one at me too. She muttered, Doesn't matter, the communists don't approve of ancestor worship. Then, she jutted her chin out at me and demanded, Are you *Goong Chan Doong*?

Laughter boomed in the room and this time I joined them. I couldn't think of the Chinese word, but remembering Roosevelt, I said, *Lor-shlu Fook*. More roaring when someone shouted out Roosevelt's nickname, *Screwed in Lucky!* Not a communist!

I observed the Ancient One in her middle country of peace and I felt calm. With both hands, I offered her tea. The Ancient One patted the bed. Her pigeon-wise eyes looked straight into mine with a pinpoint power. She reached for me and her hands were extraordinarily soft. The warmth of the cup flowed through, water to water, hand to hand. Blood.

The Ancient One lifted her cup. She said, *Today, we meet face to face. We share this cup of tea.*

I took in a deep breath and held it. The Ancient One was powerful by her position. She was on the edge of a great journey and soon she would become an Immortal.

It was what happened. I gave him life and then I gave him away. The first was not my best act and the last was not my doom.

With one exuberant calligraphic stroke, the Ancient One captured our essence; we were old and new, timeless, as she soon would be. I raised my cup and drank to her confession, to the full extract of her life. I only had two offerings: my mouth that could call her by kinship name or my palm that was her own blood and warmth.

I held my Ancient's hand till she was asleep.

* * *

BEFORE LEAVING the ancestral home, I walked through every room, touching everything, *wanting* some reminder or proof that this was real. Maybe I wanted to take something away to mark what never was and would never belong here. I looked at the dismantled bed, the old woven baskets, a cloudy mirror, all these things that belonged. I opened drawers to piles of photos, faded scarves and old republic coins, but none of those things made measure or worth of my father's beginnings here.

Ah-Seem followed me through the rooms, offering me everything I touched. Want it? Take it. Want that? Take that. Annoyed, I kept moving away from her but she stuck close as a racehorse. When I reached into the back of a drawer and pulled out a manual, I saw my father's fake name. This was his coaching book, the book of lies he'd memorized to enter America.

I held the book up and asked, How did this get here?

That? Ah-Seem shrugged. Your father sent it to the Ancient One as a message that he had arrived safely.

The ink was still vibrant, the brushed characters still velvety. On the top of the page, the questions led like flags, and on the bottom, red circles hung along the margins like anchors.

This. I held up the book and said, I want this.

Ah Seem's lower lip dragged. Take it, she said. We have no use for it.

I slipped the book into my bag and stepped outside. The girl slipped ahead and led me toward the lush fields. The air was moist, there was a menthol fragrance and soon we were at the river's edge where she climbed onto a huge flat rock, her long legs looping up like a spider's. She pointed her toes and asked me to take her picture. Even filtered through the lens, her eyes scared me. Her intent gaze was one I had seen on my father. Bold and angry. Eyes that will make you pay. Humiliation with a vengeance.

She was disappointed I wasn't using a Polaroid so I promised to send her prints but she didn't believe me and asked for my address. It was the first time she spoke directly to me and her voice was a surprise, not surly as she had used with her mother, but soft like a careful child, not used to asking and afraid of getting.

My gut reaction was to give her my post office box. When I wrote my address messily on the back of Zhen's business card, I hoped never to be surprised, I never wanted to see this child at my door holding the card like a legal document.

Ah-Seem appeared in the distance and blazed across like a field gun and then made a statement about her daughter that shocked me.

Say again? I demanded, What did you say?

Say again? she mocked me. Don't you understand what I'm saying?

I stared at her.

She stared right back and repeated in a bullying tone: Sell. We sell her. Then she threw a palm over her (golden) lower teeth as if to seal the transaction.

You're just talking, aren't you? I was surprised at how harsh my voice sounded. For the first time, I felt confident using my native dialect because finally I had something to say.

Ah-Seem gave a trembling smile and then tittered, a little loud and a little too long because she was alone in her embarrassment. I felt alone too, knowing that life was, and still is, weighed in gold. These were the things that happened. People sell people. Sons and wives, daughters and dogs. It happened then, it happened still. Only now, there are new names for it.

Ah-Seem let out an aggressive exhale and turned back toward the village. The girl looked at me as if to ask for an explanation of her mother.

So it took being in China for me to fully understand. My father's story had a proper home here. In America, his story was just talk, words strung together to color an unending fear. In China, the story was real, the story was *true*. In China, it was blood-knowledge. In the Motherland, story and feeling merged as shakily as an association between China and America. Whenever he despaired, my father threatened to go back to China. It took being in China to understand what he meant: Returning to China was returning to the Mother.

My father's story was home. The story rested where it began. The story was safe.

Finally, I understood why my Mother's mother worked at the funeral home. She had a talent for comfort. I repeated the words she spoke to each mourner and it applied now and here.

Sorrow turns several somersaults. Sorrow buries sorrow. It wasn't spirit that lived on, it was story.

Before I left the village, the elderly man who had burned the incense came to me. He spoke behind a cupped palm as if to amplify his words. *Don't add and don't take away.* Stay safe and keep us safe. Of what you see, store half in your belly. Of what you know, tell half the good and swallow half the bad. Truth is what you hold treasured in your center. Obedience is the middle, the safe position.

How perfect that China is written with the character "middle."

I WANTED to get out of China. Zhen had ordered special brushes and paper and he wanted three more days. We compromised on one more night together and he insisted on a farewell meal. I should never have trusted him. He picked the Nine Herbal Jewels, a rare foods restaurant. He thought it was extravagant but I thought it was all yuck. No way, I said when he insisted on snake. That morning, walking through the snake market, I watched men hammer nails through the snake's head and then slit razors through its belly. As if unzipped, the entrails fell out and then the thin length of meat was scraped off and the skin shimmered on the board.

Zhen insisted it was good for my system so I insisted he enjoy it. I offered to keep him company which only made him more angry. When the dish arrived, shiny and slimy, he served me a dark chunk and said, You need it. It'll boost your courage.

Boost yours! I said. I had been brave enough.

One bite, he cajoled.

I heard more command than coaxing. His set jaw told me he was ready to break something. It wasn't just his bossiness about it, but his insistence that what he thought was good, was good. At the next table, a rowdy group of Japanese businessmen were an amusing distraction. I watched a man who was so drunk, he took a nap between bites. His dinner partners never saw it because they would be turned toward each other telling a new joke just as the drunk man's head dropped onto his chest. When the others howled, the drunk man woke up in time to join in, laughing anew.

When Zhen placed the morsel into my bowl, I felt as if I and the sleepy diner were the same: unaware, unmoored, easy to trick. I tried to give the morsel back but Zhen snatched his bowl away and it fell on the table. He gave me a look that said, No Table Manners and so I muttered something back in English.

He snapped back, What's the problem? Mei Shi, no problem!

China was my problem. China was a bad joke and the joke was on me.

I'm not talking to you anymore, I said.

When the men at the next table started sloppily singing Happy Birthday in a Japanese-accented Mandarin, I realized that I was not having any fun, none.

It took being in China to feel Zhen's full "manipulative Chineseness" and for me to test my own brand of western selfishness. Collective good versus individual honesty. Zhen had hoped coming to China would give me the blood connection that would change my feeling about having a child. It backfired. Being in China only made me feel more resolute about not reversing my tubal ligation. That first night in the home village, my period came early and we walked around the night market to get Kotex (no tampons available) with my kin (the village of male elders) in tow. Though late, it was still humid and the crowds and noise made me cranky. When a gang of child-urchins started following us, Zhen yelled at a girl in dialect and it was his contempt that surprised me.

Back at the hotel, the air conditioning was so weak we left the door and windows open for a cross breeze. Zhen knew there was a different intensity in my sexual cravings as my period began. I knew it was the body remembering. He touched me and said something about the girl urchin. I pushed him away, annoyed at his indirection and there was no sex in China.

ON THE TRAIN out of Guangzhou, the dark night howled by, the hooting and clucking like barn owls in an intimate heart-to-heart. I knew I was right. It took being in China for me to believe it. I did right. I knew my choice not to have children was proof in blood.

I thought about my mother's love "in freedom" and my father's love "in history." I was like my mother, I wanted to be in love; but I was also like my father, I wanted the hard-eyed truth, the supreme loyalty.

When I wanted to know how my mother knew my father's story, her answer was so simple and direct, it shook me.

I asked, she said.

So I learned. Don't fear what you don't know.

That my father had answered her question without pause also taught me. I learned: Having no secrets gave no handle to your adversary.

MY FATHER'S STORY was never complete in America, that's why I could never let it go. But in China, his story was so common it wasn't even worth telling. Only in China, could I discover that I had mislabeled his pain for my own shame.

I left his story in the Motherland because China was its safe home.

That's when I knew. I wanted my father naturalized. Naturalization felt right. Naturalization would break the ancient old shame.

智

I BOARDED AN early flight in Hong Kong, and was seated next to a man taking his adopted Chinese daughter home. She sneaked glances at me, with eyes like magnets and soon I was holding her when the man went to the restroom. She howled when I handed her back.

My wife can't fly, the man explained, struggling as the baby's legs kicked like a propeller. I wasn't interested in hearing the story and started flipping through a magazine. But he'd been in China too long and was starved for conversation in English. He annoyed me with his long list of reasons why and how they were committed to keeping the "Chinese in the girl" (his phrase). There were plans in place, he said earnestly. Support groups, language studies, return trips to the child's hometown, and when she was ready, if she wanted, a visit to the public park where she had been found. (Or abandoned, I held my tongue).

His confession felt like an intrusion. I was glad someone was saving poor abandoned Chinese girls but it was the same old story. Someone was poor, somewhere there had been war and somehow a family could not be sustained without unspeakable sacrifice. How sad, how pitiful. I imagined the coming confusions. Though I was glad for the child, glad for the family now made complete, I was most glad I wasn't the blood mother who gave her up, or the de facto mother who would sacrifice as much only to stand second.

Finally I interrupted. Listen, you don't have to apologize or confess or even justify it and I don't have to tell you my mixed feelings about this venture. Let's just look at the good. Her.

Then I found another seat and as we lifted off from KinTak, I was surprised how low and close we flew to the skyscrapers. As I felt the jet's surge of power, I saw a woman covering her mouth in laughter. I thought of Ah-Seem and pulled out my father's coaching book. Bits of the corners crumbled like ashes in my hand and then I knew why I'd taken his book away; his life had not been lived there; that village was never home.

The heart never travels. This was my father's most elusive phrase. He used it whenever a question was too large. Now I understood, he was referring to the infinite possibilities of the *unanswerable*.

I could almost see him shaking his head, I could almost catch his askance eye. I could almost hear him sigh, which had only one translation. He was a man who trusted too much.

碧

I WATCHED IT dawn over Narita and then a second
time over the Verrazano before we landed in JFK. Unlike travel in China, everything went smoothly; I got my
luggage, no problem; I got through customs, no problem,
and then I even got a cabbie who helped with my luggage.
When he asked to smoke, I surprised myself by answering
with the expression I'd heard all over China. *Mei Shi.* No
problem, no problem.

I asked about the weather, recent crime, city scandals.
Where was he from? How did he feel being a foreigner?

Hearing myself, I was horrified, these were all questions that I hated being asked, but I couldn't stop. Where
was he from? Where did he learn his English? Did he like
being an immigrant? Was he homesick? Then I realized, I
just wanted to hear English, I wanted to feel at home.

Though he answered each question thoughtfully, he
settled it with the observation, People who are more exposed and have a larger mind, they understand more.

Do you mean, the educated class? I wanted to know.

The back of his head nodded happily. Yes, he said. Even if a person is a racist, I have to respect him because he is a human being.

I don't, I snorted. If a person doesn't like me because of my race, I hate him. Then as if that weren't bad enough, I added, And maybe forever!

I think you must be very tired, he said.

I broke up in laughter at the silly simplicity of my statement, sometimes being stupid was freeing. I picked up the *Times* on the seat and started glancing through it.

He glanced back and asked, Do you like to read?

No, I said meekly. Wrong answer again.

He shouted out exuberantly, I love reading! and then started talking about some angel named Gabriel and a sacred text. The angel delivered a bolt of cloth with writing on it to Muhammad and then commanded him to read, but Muhammad hesitated. The angel kept demanding until Muhammad was so afraid he'd be suffocated by the bolt of cloth, he confessed that he could not read. And then the angel freed him by saying: Recite!

I could barely follow the story. We hit traffic on the FDR and I looked out the window and watched a woman in the next lane applying mascara. All her features pulled downward. The city was white as a seagull and the water was a coming-green. The Verrazano came into full view like an open gate. All bridges made me feel free, welcoming and reassuring, they were my escape routes. Finally I relaxed and what I felt was relief to be out of China. I wanted to tell someone, so I just said it out loud. God! I am so glad to be home.

Excuse me?

Nothing, I said. I just needed to hear myself. I didn't want a response so I asked what he liked to read.

Oh yes! He turned around, glowing and exuberant. Yes I do! My wife reads all the time but my daughter, Fatima, complains that she has too much homework and doesn't have enough time to read.

I didn't ask where his family was because I knew soon enough he would tell.

They stay in Pakistan, he said.

I let in quiet to respect the fact.

Then his tone changed. My greatest worry is that my young Fatima won't know me.

Traffic opened up and we started moving. Before I knew it, I sat up in my seat and pushed my face up to the grated window. There was an earnestness in my voice that felt foreign yet intimate. I promise you, I said. Your daughter knows.

He glanced back quickly and I saw stillness like a spice in his eyes.

Really? he sang out.

Yes, I assured him. Your daughter already has your love, her life just has to catch up with the knowing.

His voice got low and his words came slowly. Is this true?

Yes. Very true.

I thank you. It was almost a sigh. After a long pause, he asked, And what is your story?

I surprised myself by answering. I am my father's story, I said.

He nodded, So you can understand my life.

I can, I said.

Yes. I believe you. I believe so.

At first, I mistook the softness in his voice for sadness. But I was wrong, lightness of breath was also elevation of feeling.

He turned off Seventh Avenue onto Perry. When I got out, I asked him to wait. There's something I want you to have, I said.

What? What is it? He lifted up on his heels, a kid in sneakers, his face popped again and again like champagne.

I opened my bag and pulled out my father's book and handed it to him. I kept it simple. I said, This book is my father's story. He memorized every lie in it and became another man's son. Now these lies have become his truth and his only truth is his love. I give this to you because I want it to remind you, I have heard your story. You will not need to read this, as you will not need to tell your daughter of your love. Your love already guides her.

When I handed my father's book over, I expected to feel more attachment and therefore more anxiety, but I didn't. Something lightened. Everything softened. Outside, people passed, cars stopped, the dark city bloomed around us.

He received the book with a gentle bow. In farewell, he gave me his hand and then his name: Victory.

I thanked him.

Be very happy.

Yes.

Very. The word we both repeated.

苔

I SLEPT FOR twelve hours and then packed for San Francisco. A dark suit, a pair of jeans and some T's, an umbrella and I was ready to take my father for his naturalization interview. I was groggy but jet lag was my good drug; I was rested enough but not conscious enough to be vulnerable. Jet lag would get me through my father's appointment. Yoshiye, my ex-colleague at American, listed me to fly on her companion pass. When I got onto the flight and also into first class, it was a promising beginning. Even though it wasn't yet ten, I asked for a scotch. I relaxed by watching the ramp guys in their orange stripes loading up the service carts. At takeoff, I fell asleep and woke at lunch service. I switched to wine, enjoyed the carpaccio, took a taste of mahi and then put on my eye pads.

When I woke, the flight attendants were handing out chocolates. I asked for coffee and looked out the window as the plane lifted that last bit up the peninsula. I saw the Bay, the Golden, the San Mateo Bridge. I was home.

I wasn't surprised when my name came over the PA system in a special welcome. Yoshiye was waiting for me after I deplaned. She filled me in on the gossip as we walked to her next gate and pointed out the gift shop, shouting back as she ran down the bridge way, Check out my line of travel clothing, wrinkle free, fuss free, and sexy, Yoshiye of SFO!

Seeing her made me miss being a gate agent. After boarding the passengers, I went onto the aircraft, handed the PAX manifest to the purser and then visited the cockpit to flirt and chat and clear the pilots' checklist, then I gave the final goodbye over the PA system. But my favorite part was lifting that heavy door and closing up the aircraft; I liked being the last face everyone saw.

Gatekeepers. That's what Yoshiye and I had called ourselves. The job had been my real learning college. Every day, I boarded thousands of passengers and everyone was in some sort of tight spot, many demanded I fix it. Divorce, death or just plain inept time management, I faced a thousand wrung out travelers every day and what I learned was how to face down every crisis, how to divert disastrous behavior, because if there was one place for people to go nuts, it was at the airport. Every emergency had a safety valve and what the job taught me was how to locate that essential detail in anyone. I learned to face every crisis with a moment of absolute attention.

It's a skill that has served me well even outside the terminal. In the beginning, I freaked out right alongside the desperate son trying to board a full flight to see his dying mother, the abandoned wife chasing a wayward husband, the inconsolable teenage girl. It took a lot of unruly drunks, seething lovers, but I learned how to steady my gaze, to ask what they wanted and then to calmly list their options, always leading with the worst.

Seeing Yoshiye reminded me of my talents. I could handle my father. I could do the job; I had plenty of experience. I had chauffeured many irate women and bereft widowers. Now, I had a reluctant father and I would usher him through the gates of INS. He was a problem passenger with no boarding pass, no ID. All I had to do was board him, guide him into his seat, strap him in and promise no turbulence.

No problem, I chanted. No problem, I prayed.

I took the shuttle to Avis and was on 280 by three. But Friday traffic crawled and I got off at Pacifica and took the Great Highway. I drove with the windows down, enjoying the echoing crash of the ocean waves, refreshed by the salt-snap of the sea wind. Nature was warning me to get ready. I almost stopped to walk the ruins of the old Sutro baths but decided my time would be better spent at the Buddha Bar, another sort of ruin, another aged comfort. I wound through the Presidio and then got on 17 and glimpsed the tip of the Golden Gate. I drove through Crissy Fields and enjoyed the last glow of sun on all the water vistas, the yachts lined up on the harbor, the row of swimmers doing laps along the edge of Aquatic Park. All that movement— the runners, the wind surfers and the blooming white sails of the boats—helped me breathe easier.

I drove through the whole Wharf stretch without missing a green light. Then I was on Columbus and slipping into Chinatown. Once home, I didn't waste time circling the lower alleys, didn't even bother checking the illegal spot on Beckett Lane; I just took Kearney straight into the Portsmouth garage and pulled into the first spot. On the pink column was the *zhen* ideogram and underneath that, "honesty" was written in a bold script. I thought "truth" would have been the better translation. Then I held my breath and ran up two stinky flights. When

I pushed open the heavy metal door and walked out onto Washington, the fresh wind hit hard, the sky was brittle blue and cloud free, my road ahead was unobstructed.

It was just after five but there were no Greyhound buses on the Avenue and only a few tourists strolling, their eager faces like discovery maps. Waiting to cross at the Dupont and Washington corner, a blond boy tapped me to ask about a restaurant. Instinctively, I stepped back and was surprised I still exhibited the old Chinatown fears. *Don't talk to outsiders. Don't answer questions. Don't tell your Father's name.*

I felt bad; I was mean. It was a simple question and I could have just given him information but instead, I took offense and gave him a dirty look. Tormenting tourists was a game MiMi and I had played as kids. Then, I hadn't known it was out of anger, I just felt bad that an outsider saw such a cartoon of my home: fake pagoda roofs, a Chinatown gate, rows and rows of souvenir shops, which I thought were worse than the topless bars just a few blocks away. Now, I was mad at a tourist again and I knew why. Home was a dump. Our street level was all commerce, beautified for tourists. True home was the second level, barred windows, laundry and potted plants on the fire escapes.

I looked across the street at one of Chinatown's oldest buildings. The top floor was the Chinese Benevolent Society. I could see that its wraparound veranda was packed with folding chairs, pots of dead plants, old milk crates, wooden barrels and several large steamer trunks. I could hear the wailing from the scratchy speakers; I couldn't remember the opera but I recognized Sun Ma Sze Tsang's silky voice. He was our hero; the only Chinese to hold a British license for smoking opium; chasing the dragon was his true talent.

On the street level was The Buddha Bar. I crossed, walked under the neon martini sign, pushed through the belly doors, the corduroy curtains and entered my safe cave.

The Buddha was unchanged. Walking in, I felt like I did as a kid again, coming in to look for my father. I smelled the old smells, the edge of puke and sweet vermouth, the ashy incense mixed with cigarettes, the burnt coffee and the lemons going bloaty. I saw the duct-taped barstools, the ceiling's peeling paint and the fault line crack on the mirror behind the bar. I was back in a gigantic ear where all that was said and heard and told had an ominous feel.

But MiMi wasn't there and the bartender was someone I never saw before. In Chinese, he told me she'd be back at closing. Tell her Veda came by, I said.

I got my rental out of the garage before the evening rates kicked in. It took several go-arounds before I found parking on the upper Broadway Steps and then I walked down to the news stall and sat with my father and his old cronies until closing time. I wanted to take him to a nicer place, hoping it would invite better reception to Monday's naturalization interview but we ended up across the street at Sam Wo's, which was actually best because we both felt at ease, at home, so much that we didn't even talk about it till I walked him home. By then I was so tired that I just told him about the INS appointment and I didn't react to even his noncommittal, We'll see.

WHEN I GOT BACK to the Buddha, MiMi was down bar so I dropped my stuff and sat on a stool. Every weekend and every afternoon, we came here instead of the dreaded Chinese School. We felt lucky about that and as we cut lemons, washed bar glasses and stocked beer nuts, we eavesdropped on our fathers. Inside the Buddha Bar, our fathers laughed and cursed freely. They were brave fathers who owned businesses and cars and homes and even their own true names. Once a story was told, it had to be retold. No story was finished because an ending could always be improved upon. If a father didn't like an ending, he just told it again with a better outcome. But when a father stepped outside the Buddha, he was quiet. The silent father was the safe father.

Inside, we listened in awe to our father's every rant of love, vow of revenge, every dream. But outside the Buddha, our fathers moved like fugitives and we followed them like bodyguards, shielding them with our primary English. When dark-suited men stepped up to us on the Avenue, we translated: *I call him Father. I don't know his name.*

Mimi poured coffee. How come you look like shit?

Dread, I moaned. I'm worried my Dad might freak out at INS. I moaned again. Talk about the first gate of hell.

Tell me again why are you doing this? MiMi wanted to know.

He's been talking about going back to China.

Is he sick? MiMi asked. My father did the home to China, home to croak game at the end.

I don't think so, I said.

Then, why make him naturalize? MiMi wanted to know.

My Mom. She wants him to have options. But she wants me to do the work.

When did you ever do what she wanted? MiMi asked.

I shrugged. She admitted it was her fault he lost his citizenship.

Vee, that's her guilt, not yours. Is she a Buddhist now? MiMi asked.

Sure dresses like one, I said.

I forgot, MiMi asked, how did they get together?

She met him at the Bathhouse, just after her father died. Big confusion between guilt and grief, I said.

And now? MiMi asked.

Guilt won, I said. Payback.

Big time, MiMi said.

I nodded. She finally admitted, he'd risked and he'd lost.

Why did he confess when she said she would not marry him, MiMi asked.

The worst romantic, I said.

Amazing. MiMi asked, What was it with your father?

Hope. Trust, I said.

Innocence. Inexperience, MiMi said.

That too.

To be honest, I still don't understand that Confession Program. I mean, it was supposed to be like an amnesty thing right?

Supposedly, I said. Your father confessed too, right?

Yeah, that's how his other wife, the real one, came over.

Oh, I said, that mess.

No kidding, she said. No one won.

What is your real name?

Yip, she said.

Yip?

She smiled, In Chinese that would be Yip, MiMi.

Ha!

Well, at least we can laugh, she said.

God, I said. They should call it the Confusion Program!

Yeah. MiMi laughed. Your Dad was sort of an asshole then, huh?

I nodded, Hot tempered. He's mellowed.

Mine was pretty bad, she said.

Really bad! I said.

So what else is your Mom doing besides guilt-tripping you? MiMi asked.

Same old. Still looking for herself, I tapped my glass.

MiMi poured to the rim. Where?

Calaveras County.

She raising horses? MiMi asked.

I shrugged. There are horses up there?

I swear, Vee. You're so out of it.

Nerves, I moaned. INS could be hell.

You know it will be. What I can't figure is how you got him an appointment. I mean, didn't he need to sign his own application?

I scrawled a signature on the bar and smiled.

Oh yeah, no crime there!

I'm gambling that naturalization will balance everything. He bought a fake name; why can't he buy fake security? I moaned, Dim-sum lunch, then dinner at Ilin's, INS on Monday and then it's all over.

You've got it all counted out by food, she laughed.

Yep. And I hope Ilin has a pot of shark's fin soup. Zhen told me it's packed with collagen.

Everyone knows that! MiMi said. So, how was the Motherland?

Another headache! Zhen took me to my Father's blood-mother.

She's still alive? MiMi asked.

Barely, I said.

How did he get you to go? MiMi asked.

It was a setup, I said. He didn't tell me till we got to the village gate, what could I do?

MiMi shook a fist. Kill him.

I laughed.

Down bar, the men laughed louder as they started a game of Liar's Dice. They were shouting out numbers in Cantonese as they slammed a leather cup over the thrown dice.

49!

24!

17!

So what about the blood-mother? Hey! MiMi exclaimed. Would that be your grandmother?

I nodded, She's tough.

Yeah?

And teeny.

Good combo, just like you. So what you talk about? asked MiMi.

I wasn't going to bring it up, but she did.

Bring what up?

That she sold him.

Oh, MiMi said.

No guilt, not a blink of regret, I said.

Makes sense, MiMi said. Otherwise, how could she have survived?

The old men called for a refill and MiMi moved down bar. I watched her. Her hair was cut short and from the back, she could have been a pretty boy. But what I really saw was that she was happy at the Buddha. The Buddha was her home. MiMi was better than a sister, none of the blood rivalries and all of the blood loyalty.

Can I try one more thing on you, about China, I asked.

OK, she said.

Part of me still wants to tell my Dad about meeting his mother.

Don't, MiMi said. He's already lived it.

It was the perfect answer, one I'd made in my gut but

hearing it from MiMi made it gold. It isn't worth his unhappiness, I said.

Or yours, MiMi said. You buried the story in China. Telling it would make a dead end.

No more talking, I agreed.

Celebration! MiMi reached for her reserve bottle of Beaujolais.

I raised my glass to the statue of Buddha behind the bar. MiMi toasted to the dead.

To growing older and wiser! My first sip had a victorious taste and I felt strong.

There was a shout and I saw two leather-clad tourists at the door. They intoned, English? English?

I didn't smile but maybe MiMi did. The men walked in, cradling helmets. The shorter one took the seat near the service shelf and the taller, bald one sat next to me. He leaned in too close and told too much without my asking: his record business, his wife, his infant daughter. His pointy shaved head gleamed and so did his silver bicuspids, which surprised me enough to ask, Are you poor?

The way he shook his head, I knew he hadn't understood. So I asked, Your teeth. Why didn't you get gold?

He looked like how a guy looks when offended, but confused about how to react, just shook his head as if impotency were only a headache.

You look tired, he said through clenched teeth.

I smiled with mine and said, I am.

The Short One was telling MiMi about their twelve-hour ride up from Joshua Tree.

Yeah? I asked. Not as bad as your twenty-two-hour flight, a stopover in Frankfurt, to Mozart International, in Salzburg right? I saw the Short One glancing at the door, a getaway fear in his eye.

Relax! MiMi said. She worked the airlines for years

and can key your destination from your manner and speech.

I pointed at his backpack and said, You shouldn't leave your tags on.

MiMi served up their beers. What is it about guys and road trips?

The desert was tremendous, the Bald One said.

Tremendous. That was a word I hated, too touristy.

The Bald One was talking about the extremes, the rocky landscape, the raw heat, the coyotes, the glow of cactus. He smiled and his silver canines flashed like sparklers.

Why there? MiMi asked.

The Short One said, We made a film about our pilgrimage to Gram Parsons' place of demise.

Demise. Another word that annoyed me.

Is the police tape still around the hotel room? MiMi asked.

It was, they nodded.

What is it about Parsons that got you into the 120 degree heat, MiMi wanted to know.

I like his free spirit, the Short One stuttered, His, his . . . how you say? His wild disregard?

The Bald One started humming, then said San Francisco feels like Sin City.

Is he popular with the Chinese? the Short One asked.

MiMi said, One of our own wrote his biography.

Really? the Short One piped up. Can we interview him?

I don't think so, MiMi said.

You mean Ben? I asked.

MiMi smacked her lips. Now there's an example of the perfect Chinese guy.

Why? Because he's in with rock and roll or because he's at East-West News?

Because he's the second son, MiMi said. First sons

think they're the Buddha and last sons are snot-babies, but middle sons are the dream because they've been kicked around, like daughters.

True! I shouted.

The Bald One leaned in so close, I could almost feel his silver teeth piercing, I could almost smell his leech mouth ready to eat. Then I ignored MiMi's look and went outside with him. We had a smoke and then I took him up into Old Spanish Alley, into that wide entryway by Ching's barber shop and I fucked him just for the hell of it. We came back for another drink but I said No to going on with him.

MiMi served coffee with the last call and then I helped her close up, washing out the glasses, restocking the beer, emptying and cleaning out the coffee machine, putting the lemons away, wiping down the bar and sweeping up the peanut shells. She counted out the till as I stacked the chairs and stools. She turned off the lights, locked up and then we left. We rode in silence down deserted Kearney, onto Market where the night views were unwrapping.

He sort of gleamed, I said. I thought about the Bald One's coldness, his silver teeth, his prickly head, his protruding clavicles and I shivered. He even sort of had a metal taste, he was so clammy, it was sort of scary, I said.

Maybe you wanted to be scared, MiMi said. Then she just drove. Downtown was empty and along the streetcar tracks, the night view was yellow lights and metal tracks, with only an occasional street corner transvestite, all glittering gold teeth and lamé platform shoes.

When we turned onto Sloat, the road widened and MiMi asked, You telling Zhen?

What for? My harsh tone surprised me. MiMi's genius was how she loaded up a question. I had answered before I really knew what MiMi was asking, but the truth was disheartening. No applied to both, to confessing about the bald guy and to not untying my tubes.

She pulled into her garage, cut the engine and turned to me. So, Love dies?

Does love? I wondered. I loved him enough. So why didn't I want to give him what would make him happy? I looked at MiMi, mesmerized by how the tips of her hair glowed just before she flicked off the headlights. She wouldn't look at me, she just said, Do me a favor, will you? Then she got out of the car and gave the door a hard sucking slam.

What? I followed her up the stairs, demanding, What? But she waited till she got to the top before throwing her scold over her shoulder. Surprise me sometime, Vee.

I never have? I trailed her into the apartment. Never? I asked again, dropping my stuff and zipping out of my boots. She ignored me but I followed her into the kitchen and while she filled the kettle and lit the stove, I kept asking, Well?

She turned and let her hard eye fire onto me. Vee, you never think, you just do.

I sat down. Something about her tone scared me, so I went right to the thing that I felt most guilty about in our relationship—June 18th. After weeks of fog, summer arrived early, sudden and glorious and the whole city burned in celebration. Our fathers were in Reno overnight. We went to our secret cove on Bakers' Beach, suntanned and smoked some gold from Kona. We watched the tide coming in, the tide leaving. The sun set before we even thought about heading back to Wayne Alley. Then we went to Sam Wo's for an order of tomato beef chow mein, Sun Wah Kue's for a custard pie. At the Buddha, MiMi asked Pegeen for a bottle of Beaujolais from the Buddha.

So we had the whole evening ahead of us and we were

celebrating turning eighteen. My defenses were down and a series of connections I would normally have thought odd, I found interesting.

Earlier that week, I'd passed a parked car and seen the driver slumped over the steering wheel and reported it to the police. They took down my information, but I forgot about it till the phone rang just as MiMi and I sat down to feast. The caller identified himself as being from the Vallejo Street precinct and that he was coming by with some questions about my report. We thought it was weird, but when there was a knock, I let the guy in. He turned out to be a cadet cop with serious problems and it went really badly, ending with MiMi getting raped. Nothing happened to me. I was in the other room the whole time. I always blamed myself. MiMi never did. She said she had something tangible to "get over" whereas my guilt was something more intangible, something I kept "doing" to myself. That was MiMi, a gem person.

Mi? Do you ever think about it? I knew I shouldn't bring it up but I couldn't help myself. When she gave me her, Do-we-have-to look, I stopped her.

I let the guy in! I said.

MiMi screamed, Will you PLEASE stop it? I never blamed you because it was never your fault. You want to know the truth?

I'm not sure, I mumbled.

I was more mad that you stayed with my asshole brother as long as you did.

I know, I said. But he "saved" us.

Veda! she pleaded. He just happened to come by, wanting to get some of that Kona. You feel guilty about something else.

I know it sounds crazy, but the way I lined it up is like this, I owed and I felt that if I could straighten your brother out, it was repayment.

Oh Man! MiMi slammed the cabinet shut, threw the mugs down in front of me and said, Could you please stop with the retribution and obligation crap, we're not playing that payback game OK? I don't have to give you a horse on your birthday and I don't want you sending over two studs on mine. You don't owe me and I don't owe you. We're friends because we want to be and if we become enemies, it'll be about something real. Not guilt, not regret.

I mulled that over.

She leaned in close, her slow voice threatening. Do you want me to be honest?

Not really, I mumbled.

Then her eyes glistened like carp. She asked, I always wanted to know, why didn't you leave? You could have.

I never thought of it, he had you in the other room, I said.

The kettle's screech broke our quiet.

Her eyes were as clear and direct and relieved as that night when we were released from the Vallejo precinct. Thank you, she said.

My heart stopped. Two simple words wrapped in a cloud. I had never heard her voice so safe. Everything was still. I listened to the kettle whistling like a siren from some god. Then I said, Besides, he tied me up, remember?

MiMi's laugh broke us out of the past. This story was always about friendship, she said. That's why I couldn't see you for a while, I just needed a break; it wasn't you, it was the story.

You were protecting the friendship, I said.

I nodded.

Our training, MiMi said. We learned to protect our parents. I never told my Father either but maybe my dumb old UCB brother did.

Rodney? How is the Useless Chinese brother? I wanted to know.

In rehab.

Again?

Ruined by Mother love, MiMi said. That night he did good by us but it won't ever make up for the grief he put Dad through. Maybe my Dad forgave him before he died but I won't. Then she turned a hard eye on me. But this isn't about him. It's not even really about this Zhen guy. I don't need to tell you how stupid it would be to be "spending time" with a Chinese guy and letting him think of a future if you have no plans for it. Vee! Are you nuts? He's Chinese, he's Chinese from China! Didn't you say he was an only son?

Of an only son, I added.

Big trouble, MiMi said.

I guess.

Let me ask you this then, Do you ever think of breaking up with him?

All the time, and not because I don't love him, it's just reflex, like my Mom.

MiMi rolled her eyes. You're always running.

I can't help it, I said. My mother was always on the run, my father wanted to be that Immortal bird, flying forever and my Grandmother hoarded the plots by the road for her favored dead. What about your father? Remember how he always took the aisle seat at the movie theater?

Yes or no? You know what I'm asking.

I stammered, It's my nature to always want "out." I don't know any other way to be "in."

Sure, yeah, MiMi said.

Don't buy it? I tried smiling.

Nope. MiMi rolled her eyes and then asked, He wants a family, right?

I nodded.

Would you reverse the procedure, for him?

No, I blurted.

Well, you wasted no time answering that one, she said. You talk shit about obligation but you won't do anything. I don't know this Zhen, don't know if I'd even like him, but I know this: You owe him. Give him some considera-tion. MiMi leaned forward, You know what I mean. Don't let him misunderstand. Face what you can do. Be honest about what you can't do. Then, tell him. Talk and tell, this is the story. You and him, here. Not that old China story, not our cop story, but this one with this Zhen.

I laughed but there was no relief, just that hard burp of truth of the past throwing up on the present. The good of talking to MiMi was that I trusted her, talking to her was like talking to myself, the bad was that she talked back and said stuff I didn't want to hear.

You're smarter than that, Veda. He wants a family and he wants it with you. Have you asked him how he might feel without a child?

Do I have to? I whined.

What if he answers Yes? Would you trust him?

I shrugged again, Probably not.

I wouldn't, MiMi said. Recipe for bitterness. If that's your answer, then let him go find someone who can give him this happiness. You're the wrong girl. Be honest with him, be honest for yourself. Be like your mom.

I could feel my tears welling up from deep, the sob-bing coming on. I swallowed.

Remember how my father used to talk about the two types of wailers at the bar?

I nodded.

One was the sort whose weeping could stain bamboo and the other was the wah-wah of a boy who'd lost his cricket.

I chirped.

All I'm saying is that he seems the kind of man who believes peace comes from family, that for him, children make the peace, MiMi said.

Maybe we can adopt? I ventured.

You're avoiding, MiMi said. Why are you so against family?

Then I remembered Victory. What is the worth of family?

ILIN WAS ALWAYS the one I trusted. When I asked her to authorize my permission sheet for my tubal ligation, she couldn't read it, but looked at it as if deciphering something more significant. Such anger is harmful, she said.

I don't care, I said. I never want to be a mother.

She said, You can't know that now. You can't know what can open up for you when you have a golden time with a man.

I do, I said. I saw her eyes tearing up and I remembered that she'd lost a baby. It's my only protection, I said.

What are you protecting yourself from? she wanted to know.

I don't want to be a mother, I said. Out loud, it sounded pretty stupid.

Her face paled as if I'd slapped her. She talked then, in a formal way that felt harsh. I didn't understand every word, I only approximated her meaning from her tone.

Don't make my mistakes. What was old hurt revisited? Was it the body trying to save something so ancient it had almost lost its name? I was like you, consumed by the same passion. I sold myself into this marriage to achieve one goal. I wanted to find my Uncle and I wanted to damn him. Hate drove me. Anger gripped me. I refused my own living until I

fulfilled this promise. But when I met him, my desire for rec-
ompense was like a weak whistle. I had believed passion was
the absence of fear, but I would learn it was only the presence
of unreasonable blame.

You will do what you want, but I plead: Ask yourself,
Who is this promise to? Remember, that your first debt is to
yourself.

I pushed my form forward.

What holds you in this fury? Her voice cracked.

I assumed she was thinking about the baby she lost. I
didn't want her to ask about Noland so I signed and then
handed her the pen.

Her eyes were steady, her hand was firm. Let's not tell
your father, she said.

I don't care. My voice cracked like when I was scared.

Look at me, she said. You are not forcing my hand.
When I lost my child and was brimming with desire to be
loved in need, you were given to me. I was your Stand-in
Mother, but I will never stand in the way of your happiness. I cannot protect you from your own youthful fearlessness.

Here, I tapped on the dotted line.

Listen to what I have to tell you. Her voice was steady
and her eyes were hard.

I waited.

In life, surprise is the blood we let. I will give you the
permission that will allow you to shut the door to your
nature.

I watched her put pen to paper. I watched how she
made her careful letters, the full bodied I, the brush like a
hat over the i, the legs of the Z that dangled below the line.
Then she pushed the sheet back toward me, clicked the pen
and put it on the table.

I saw my name; I saw her name.

Thank you. My voice sounded as far away as if I was on one end of the Broadway tunnel, murmuring.

Then Ilin said, Remember what I tell you now. When you feel regret, when you need forgiveness, know that you can give it to yourself.

eternity 11

MIMI WAS the only person I ever told about Victory. I never wanted to dilute the story with another telling. When MiMi started crying, I was stunned. I was silent when she apologized. When she said, I'm just moved by his story.

I said, Yes.

Victory was all our fathers.

MY FATHER LIVED his story, tenacious.

When my mother told me his story, it was the only time I saw her tender. She offered his story as an apology for all that I might not understand about him, a door to forgiving. The girl in her was telling me why she almost loved the boy.

Then I remembered Grandmother's words: Telling was not necessarily loving. Once spoken, words take on a power beyond time. She taught me to weigh my words.

Only the dead forgot, only the dead had the power to take the stories away, only the dead truly forgave.

Grandmother was right. *Stories became our ancestors, our Gods of memory.*

These memories prepared me for taking my father to his naturalization interview. Tomorrow, I would take my father across another river.

THE CHINESE CONFESSION

PROGRAM

GN 00302.970 Chinese "Confession" Cases

A. RULE

SSI claims personnel must be aware of the Chinese "confession" procedure and give due consideration to it in evaluating the INS arrival record as evidence of age.

B. BACKGROUND: RESTRICTIVE LAWS

Because of severely restrictive and discriminatory Federal immigration laws (e.g., the Chinese Exclusion Act of 1882), many persons of Chinese ancestry born abroad were able to enter the U.S. only by assuming fictitious identities.

Chinese immigrants who entered the U.S. before the passage of the Exclusion Act could remain; however, their families could not join them and, if they left the U.S., they could not reenter. Persons of Chinese ancestry who had been born in the U.S. could leave and reenter the U.S., but their spouses could not join them. Children of such individuals (and certain classes of individuals not born in the U.S., such as professionals, students, authors, artists, etc.) could enter the U.S. if unmarried and under age 16. Merchants were excepted from the general rule and could bring in unmarried children under age 21. Individuals in the excepted groups were required to prove their exempt status each time they entered the U.S. and to retain this status while in the U.S.

C. CREATION OF FICTITIOUS IDENTITIES

INS carefully documented arrival, departure, reentry, etc., concerning all Chinese. This fact and the fact that the Chinese Government had no public records of birth, aided the Chinese immigrants in devising ingenious means to circumvent the laws. There were various combinations of opportunities for smuggling relatives, friends, clients, etc., into the U.S. through use of fictitious identities as children of the Chinese "travelers" authorized to reenter the U.S.

D. CHINESE "CONFESSION" PROCEDURE

In 1956 INS instituted a program to eliminate the creation of "paper families" by Chinese immigrants. The purpose of this "confession" program was to encourage and assist all aliens (not just Chinese) who illegally entered the U.S. to adjust their status to that of an alien lawfully admitted for permanent residence, which in turn paved the way to naturalization. The program extended into the 1960s.

The Chinese applied the term "Hon Pak" ("To Confess") to the new program.

Confession
Hon Pak

Hon Pak is the word of a generation of men who confessed, who surrendered truth, *"blank and true."*

智

M Y FATHER WASN'T downstairs when I pulled into
Wayne Alley so I hit the horn. It felt good and the
second honk felt even better. But as he came down the stairs,
I saw the whole vexing day written on his face and I felt
dread. He got in with a big sigh but wouldn't look at me.

Good morning to you! I said.

He grunted.

Troublemaker, I muttered. Did you study? I asked.

He pulled out his *Manual of 100 Naturalization Questions* and squinted at the first page. When I asked if he
wanted to go back for his glasses, he shook his head and I
noticed that the hole in his ear had scabbed like a burn
scar. So what if I flunk? he asked.

I backed out of the alley and he bumped against the
door. What else did you study besides history and government? I asked.

That's all there is, right?

What about civic obligation and responsibility? I
queried.

He thumbed through the manual and said, There's nothing about that in here.

Think about it, I said. They'll ask, Why do you want to be an American?

Not scared then, not scared now, he said.

Nothing to lose then, less to lose now, I mumbled. The Number 55 Sacramento squeaked like a run-over rat. Then my father stuck his head out the window and yelled, Edso Lim, get out of the street!

I braked and watched a group of children cross the street. One girl clutched her books protectively to her chest and I remembered my father's coaching book and thought, If he could memorize three hundred lies to become another man's son, he'd better repeat one hundred facts to become an American.

Young Miss! Edso pushed his face inside the car. Where you taking your father?

INS, I said.

You deport him? Edso shouted.

You come too, Edso, they give you a free ticket to China! my father shouted.

I started inching forward.

Edso backed away from the window and waved. Good bye! Good luck!

My father chuckled, That Fool is still scared.

The Number 55 started up and the car rolled forward. I turned into the garage and parked. We walked in silence to 100 Sansome Street. Immigration and Naturalization was embossed in gold letters above the double doors, making what already felt official, look commercial too. I got him through security (no incident) rode up the express elevator to the nineteenth floor (no problem) and signed him in (no struggle). But when we entered the small white waiting room, his eyes twitched back and forth like a

switchblade, so I picked a seat far away from anyone. On
the window sill, a dove cooed. I gave him a *National Geo-
graphic* and immersed myself in an article about memory
loss in *AARP*. He changed seats, dropped his *Manual* and
sighed like a slaughtered pig, but I ignored him. Let him
sit with his own fear, I decided. I would not give him a
stage to perform his whiny opera.

In the far corner, two women whispered. Across from
them, a dark-suited man sat alone, his briefcase wide open
on his lap. A large boy-man in a red flannel shirt and stiff
soiled jeans was pacing the room. He had a soft face and
his gray-haired parents watched him, still as pigeons.

A male officer opened the door and called out names
and the two women rose and followed him inside. A
woman officer walked an interviewee out. The interviewee
asked in halting English, not once but twice, When is the
ceremony?

Sir, we will review your case. The woman officer's
firm tone was not encouraging.

When? The interviewee asked.

The officer exhaled, a quick air puff like the eye test
for glaucoma. You'll get a letter.

I hoped we would not be assigned to her. The large
son paced by and I saw that his feet were too big for his
frame, which explained why he kept moving. Whenever
he stood still, he looked like he might topple over. His fists
beat against his thighs as he continued to fabricate his
story: But I wasn't arrested in California. In Oregon, DUI
is not a felony, it's only a misdemeanor! The mother nodded. The father suggested, Tell them it was the medication,
you're sick, the medication is for your manic depression.

I felt resentful having to listen to his idiotic lies and I
was just about to say something when the door opened.

Jack Moon Szeto?

My heart sank, it was the woman officer. My father and I approached her. She barred my passing with her clipboard. Her nose, brow and chin formed a pyramid. Behind her frameless glasses, her eyes were youthful, almost mischievous but when she spoke, her voice was stern. You can't come in, she said to me.

She didn't like me. But I was ready for this. I wore flat shoes, monotone colors, and had tied my hair back, I could have been going to one of my Grandmother's wakes. Then I got into my gate agent mode. I smiled as I did when faced with an irate, life-late, life-worn steerage PAX wanting an upgrade. I asked for permission: May I tell you something?

She didn't say no, but she squinted like she was trying to erase me from her vision. So I began, My father doesn't speak much English. Then I paused. Her lip pulled down and I read the question on her face: And how long has he been here?

Forever, I wanted to say, but I held my tongue. I'd answered this question so many times, it was no longer a question but the answer to all that was lost and hopeless in his life, so I circumvented her accusation. I told her I had flown in from New York to accompany my father to his naturalization interview. I wanted to translate for him. Again, I asked for permission. Would that be all right?

I will have to check with my Supervisor, she said. Then she took in a large suck of air as if to say, Don't hold your breath. When she turned, her Joan of Arc haircut softened her. I saw that young dip at her nape and knew she had sweetness in her. I took it as a good sign that she escorted us into her office. I sat down, relieved we'd passed through the first gate. The window looked out on the Transatlantic Building and beyond, I saw the gray stitch of the Bay Bridge and thought about why I favored the Bay over the Golden. The Bay was like an industrial track that stretched across the harsh waters like a real road out, not like the Golden Gate, which was frail, with its high-wind closings and cable beautification upkeep. I pointed to the Bay and my father nodded.

The Officer returned. The Officer seemed more severe. All right, she said. But you might hear things you don't know about, are you ready for that?

There was no time for worry. Yes, I said.

Please raise your right hand, the Officer directed.

My father raised his, too, as if this was a familiar ritual. We swore to tell the truth.

My translation strategy was to end with the key words because those were the words I wanted my father to repeat. I would keep a flat inflection because any rise in tone might excite him and any low tones might make the Officer suspicious.

We were a triangular confessional. The Officer asked the questions and I translated; my father answered and I translated back. With both eyes focused on me, I felt like the interrogated one.

The Officer asked, What year were you born?

I translated, Year of birth?

1935. Year of the Long March, my father answered.

The Officer asked, What was your port of entry?

I translated, What port?

He answered, San Francisco.

The Officer studied several pages of his file and then looked directly at him and said in Chinese, *Goong Chan Doong?*

I was shocked that she used the Chinese for a Communist. Before I could translate, my father threw his head back and laughed and I worried, laughing was not good.

I translated, Are you a Communist?

My father shook his head like a wet dog's.

The Officer said, I need him to answer.

I translated, The Officer needs to hear your answer. Yes or No?

No! No *Goong Chan Doong*.

The Officer checked off something on her form, and then asked, Were you ever in deportation hearings?

Deport. That word sent me right back to the Buddha Bar. I was a child again watching every father's face freeze up.

Deport? My father repeated the word in a hushed voice.

No, not now! I panicked but couldn't think of the Chinese word so I asked, Did the FBI try to kick you out? FBI was another bad word choice.

No, never! He shook his head.

The Officer asked, Did you ever go in front of a deportation judge?

I wanted to avoid the word deport so I translated, Did a judge call you?

He looked confused so I reached over to reassure him but touching his empty sleeve gave me a shock.

I need an answer, the Officer insisted.

I knew the right answer, I knew the true answer. But I also knew it wasn't my right to answer for him.

Then, to my surprise, the Officer spoke directly to me. She said, He may not have known it, but he was under deportation hearings.

I took that as permission. We're talking the Chinese Confession Program, right?

The Officer dropped her guard. I never even heard about this till just ten minutes ago.

I saw her irises, a flicker of blue as if the sky beyond had come in through the glass, like grace. She shut my father's file. That was a difficult period, she said.

I nodded. Out the window, I watched the cars on the Bay Bridge inching forward like tracks on a zipper.

The Officer glanced at my father. He smiled back and then saluted. I looked at them both, feeling a battling of loyalties.

Behind the partition, a man cleared his throat repeatedly.

Listen, she said. At his age, we won't throw him out. Then she resumed the interview. Ask, Were you ever arrested?

I asked my father, Were you ever in jail?

He answered, No.

She pursued it. Did you ever commit a crime for which you were not arrested?

I asked, Did you break the law?

He answered again. No.

She persisted. When you were in China, did you break Chinese law?

I asked: In China, Did you break the law?

He looked perplexed and he answered No.

Ask him again. Did you commit a crime in China for which you were not caught?

I asked, In China, did you break the law and no one knew?

No.

I saw his eyes flicker and I worried.

Ask, How many wives did he have?

I asked, How many wives?

He answered: One.

Ask him again: In the world, how many wives did he have?

I asked: All over the world, how many wives?

My Father answered in his real voice, harsh, impatient. Only one. Why does she ask everything twice?

The Officer shuffled through the thick file. I saw blacked out sections on several pages. The yellowed tissue carbon copies rustled like the shells of dried insect wings. When her eyes stopped on his empty sleeve, I had to hold my breath to resist throwing out a preemptive explanation.

Let's finish, she said. Ask him, Will he be a good American?

I asked.

He answered, Of course.

Ask, Will you obey American law?

I asked.

He nodded, Right.

Ask, From which country did America fight for independence?

I asked my Father, but I went blank, what was the answer?

England! my father shouted.

The Officer laughed too and I asked permission to praise him. She nodded assent and I said, You're good, Dad!

My father beamed, victorious.

Then the Officer gathered all the papers and folded her hands over the thick stack. Listen, she said.

I held my rejoicing.

He has two names, the Officer said. Ask him which one he wants to keep.

I asked, Which name do you want?

Both. Both names are mine, he said.

I report that.

He has to choose, she said.

Choose, I told him.

He repeated, I want both.

Choose, I bared my teeth. You can only have one.

We sparred with our eyes, swallowing all we could not say.

What is he saying? she asked.

I appealed to her with a troubled face. He can't choose, I said.

Her smile was sincere, but stiff.

My father set his jaw and I felt locked into some middle jail. That's when I understood. His expression was one that had baffled me all my life, and it was also the one that I had seen all over China. The enduring, the tenacious, the vexing face. That's when I realized, he always wore a face that could go both ways. Loyalty was in the moment. That's when I accepted that I was the one who had to surrender.

I took a deep breath and just then my father averted his eyes, permitting me.

I chose Jack Moon Szeto. I chose his fake name, the name he lived half his life with, the name he made with his own sweat, the name he surrendered for love, the name that made him true.

acknowledgments

I thank the American Academy of Arts and Letters Rome Prize, the Lannan Foundation and the Lila Wallace-Reader's Digest Writers' Award for their generous support. I am indebted to my agent, Neil Olson, for his loyal, astute reading of all manuscripts, especially his recall of those lost and forgotten, which saved and shaped this work. I thank my publisher, Robert Miller, for his belief, Will Schwalbe for his dedication and my editor, Zareen Jaffery, for her bold and serene eye.

I am grateful to Patricia Mulcahy for her camaraderie on the page and her unvexable life-spirit.

A great many people were generous to the life of this book by offering kindness, knowledge, wit and trust. Time in their presence was golden and my gratitude is unending. To the named, for enduring friendship, Colleen Chikahisa, Diana Chow, Gil Cohen, Pamela Crossley, Rosa and Ivo Del Borgo, Antonella De Muti, Han Feng, Paul Gervais,

ACKNOWLEDGMENTS

Sarah Glasscock, Patti Hiramoto, Lisa Hsia, Barbara Klar, Peggy Levison, Anson Louie, Wendy and Dr. Nelson Lowe, Katherine McNamara, Cathleen Morawetz, Mamma Pia, Diane Y. Takeshita, Anne Twitty, Peternelle Van Arsdale, Jack Wesley and Rosina Lee Yue. To the unnamed, and to the dearly missed, Hannah Green, Alison Lasley, Elizabeth Murray, the Aunt who embroidered and the Grandmother who sang me her wedding songs.

To Ner, for the world behind each word, for love.